HELL HATH NO SCORN

Hell Hath No Scorn

A novella

by

JOSHUA LAKHAMRAJU

Adelaide Books
New York / Lisbon
2021

HELL HATH NO SCORN
A novella
By Joshua Lakhamraju

Copyright © by Joshua Lakhamraju
Cover design © 2021 Adelaide Books

Published by Adelaide Books, New York / Lisbon
adelaidebooks.org

Editor-in-Chief
Stevan V. Nikolic

For any information, please address Adelaide Books
at info@adelaidebooks.org
or write to:
Adelaide Books
244 Fifth Ave. Suite D27
New York, NY, 10001

ISBN: 978-1-954351-75-2

Printed in the United States of America

Contents

CHAPTER 1

It was a sunny Friday afternoon as a man entered into the lobby of a hotel and straight towards the front desk. A couple of women were standing behind the counter. One of them noticed the man's presence. "Good afternoon" she smiled. "Good afternoon", he echoed, "I have a reservation for a room 238. Name is Joe Denna." The receptionist looked through the computer. "Oh yes, here you are! Yes Mr. Denna, here is your room card, and we are glad to have you staying with us." The man then smiled and nodded before heading outside to retrieve his luggage from his car.

For Ann Noyd, this day was just like any other day. Checking the guests in and out, answering the phone, and ordering amenities like extra towels for the guests whenever they asked. But although other people may find this line of work boring, Ann found it fun as it allowed her to interact with different people. The 35-year old, who had long black hair that sparkled in the sun, had been working full time in this same job for more than twelve years, and had been given recognition and rewards at work like pay raises and Employee of the Week, Month, or Year several times.

The luxury hotel that Ann worked at was located in an affluent, downtown part of the major city. Prominent people like heads of state, business leaders, celebrities, and many more would often reside her. Ann often had the honor of meeting such people, even if it was briefly and primarily at the front desk when they were checking in or out. She had often considered asking them for an autograph or selfie, but company policy forbad that in order to give the guests privacy protection.

Today, Ann had no such luck in getting such chance encounters with such people. She had no clue who Joe Denna was. A google search turned up several Joe Dennas. None of them seemed prominent or outstanding in any way. But Ann decided not to mind, as she savored the opportunity to meet someone she had never known before. For Ann, even a short and simple conversation with an average nobody was better than having nobody to talk to all day.

Of course, hardly a day would go by when, if there was no guest to talk to, she could talk with her coworkers. She was on good terms with them, but she much preferred conversing with her female coworkers than with then men. As with any workplace, lots of people get on and off the payroll. Whenever one of her female coworkers would leave, Ann would often feel at least just a little sad to see them go. Whenever it was a male, Ann would often openly express sadness towards him for leaving. But secretly, she was elated and relieved to see him go.

The front desk and guest relations department was largely comprised of women. Ann always felt secure whenever she was around them. Any male who joined the team would stay for at most a few months before leaving. There were lots of other men employed by that hotel, but most of them worked in other departments, particularly the valet and restaurant, most of which tended to be male-dominated. "Thank goodness I don't have to work in any of those departments" Ann would tell herself privately, "I would probably lose my mind over in those muscle-bound, possibly fast-paced environments."

As the day came to an end, so did Ann's shift. The rush hour traffic was heavy, as it usually was this time of year, especially in downtown. Cars were honking, and the occasional siren would blare. Whenever there was an accident or a crime-related emergency. Ann was no stranger to this traffic mess. She had a hard time getting onto the road as the intersection where the hotel was located was blocked by traffic. After waiting impatiently for several minutes, Ann finally managed to squeeze into the traffic. But once on the road, Ann was again stuck with all the cars backed up for miles.

"Could all this be because of an accident, or is it just busy as usual?" she asked herself. The only way she could tell the real cause of the traffic buildup was whenever she heard a siren blaring, and then she saw the flashing lights of an emergency vehicle in her rearview mirror. She hated whenever it was indeed an emergency, as it only added to the crowded roads. Tonight, there was no emergency on her side of the road, although she could hear sirens blaring in the faraway distances heading in the opposite lanes. "Thank God it ain't it tonight" she sighed.

Several more minutes went by before Ann could enter the highway. But as soon as she got onto the entry lane, it was packed all the way to the intersection, and Ann had to wait even more. Finally, she got her chance, and slowly crawled onto the highway. But once on the highway, it was also crowded. As with the downtown traffic, Ann would often hope that the traffic jam was the result of the day being busy as usual, and not the result of an accident. Once again, there were no signs of any emergency vehicles around. "Yup, it's busy as usual alright" she mused as she drove at a snail's pace.

It took Ann more than half an hour to finally exit the highway and onto to a quiet, much less-crowded road. Minutes later Ann pulled into the driveway of her house in the suburban neighborhood. Once she arrived, she saw a familiar car that was also parked on the driveway. "Well, you know who that is and what that means" she sighed as she got out of her car and made her way towards the front door. The lights outside were on, so Ann had no trouble navigating her way to the front door and opening it up. She could also see that the inside lights were on, and someone was moving around and about from inside the house. Once inside, she saw a familiar person sitting on the living room couch.

"Hello Thad" she sighed as she stared at him.

"Hi Ann!" said her husband as he walked over to hug her. "It has been a while now, hasn't it?"

"Yes" muttered Anne as she tepidly embraced him, "it certainly has been a while. Like, only about 12 hours."

Thad chuckled. "Every time you're away, it almost feels like an eternity. Even if it is just for a few hours. But I always look forward to having you back."

"I feel the same way" she sighed as she stared at his eyes with a fake smile.

After Ann had changed into her night clothes, they both sat down to dinner that Thad had made before she arrived. "How has your day been?" asked Thad.

"Great, as usual. Nothing out or the ordinary. No VIPs today. Hopefully, I will get to see one on Monday when I return to work." Ann paused, and then smiled. "But my good friends will always be there, no matter if any VIPs visit or not."

"I'm glad you are enjoying your job, darling. Sometimes I wonder if you ever get bored of it, having to perform the same duties every day, seeing the same bosses and coworkers every day. It all seems monotonous to me."

"I would agree with you, if the work environment was anything but friendly. I cannot think of a single boss or coworker who has been a jerk. At least, they have not been a jerk to me. I guess they have too much respect for me than anyone else does."

Ann had said this in a passive-aggressive manner, and Thad had picked up on that. He paused for a moment before chuckling, "Except of course yours truly!"

"Yes, of course, you" replied Ann dryly with another forced smile, "because there is no one else in this entire world who loves and respects me more than you."

The next morning, which was Saturday, Ann got ready to go out to the mall with her girlfriends. Thad was a little disappointed that he could not spend quality time with her, as he had been yearning for that opportunity for a long time. "Sweetheart" he told her as she was looking for her car keys, "I don't want to sound like a crybaby, but I really think we should go out somewhere some time together. We haven't done that in, oh, I don't know, weeks, months maybe. I know how much you want to be around your friends, but I want to be with you, just for one day at least."

Ann was quite irritated by Thad's request. "Selfish son of a bitch just wants to make my life miserable, as if he hasn't done so already" she thought to herself. But instead, she smiled put her hands on his shoulders, and kissed him lightly on the cheeks. "I know just how you feel, dear, but I already promised them I would be with them all day. You and I both know that going back on our promises is never a good idea. They would never forgive if I were to dump them, even if it were just once or even if it were for a good reason."

"I understand" replied Thad, "but it seems as though you are far happier being with them than you are with me. I just hope that you still love me as much as I love you."

"Of course I love you, Thad, but you need to understand that, women like myself need time off for ourselves to be together. You may not specifically understand what I am talking about, but I am sure that you are smart enough to realize that there are times to be with one's family, and then there are times to be with one's friends. Today is the day that I am to be with my friends."

"Fine then, today you be with your friends. But tomorrow, you can perhaps hang out with me. Is that a good idea for you? Because I am off work all of tomorrow."

Ann averted her eyes from Thad for a few seconds as she stalled to come up with an answer that she felt would satisfy him. "Well, I guess I could hang out with you tomorrow. But I need to think about it today. I will let you know after I return, but I won't promise you anything."

With a brief hug and kiss, Ann grabbed her keys, exited the door, and drove away. "Phew!" she sighed as she was on the road, "I thought he would keep interrogating me until I gave him my friends' names and Social Security numbers. That son of a bitch can't stop sticking his nose into places where he doesn't belong. He keeps getting on my nerves like he has nothing better to do. The sooner I get rid of him, the better!"

Ann grumbled about Thad until she arrived at the mall as planned. She met her girlfriends, Laura, Lisa, and Sally, at the main entrance as they had planned. They spent just about the entire day there, where they shopped, dined, and talked about whatever they were interested.

"How is Tad, or however you say his name?" asked Lisa.

Ann chuckled, "It is Thad. And he is doing just fine. He does, however, seem to be very sad whenever I spend the weekends with my girlfriends, including you three. And he wants to spend more quality time with me. And I feel the same way.

I love him so much, that I would not want to be with anyone else besides him at any given time."

"So what are you doing here, then?" asked Sally as the other two slightly snickered.

Ann was caught off-guard by this unexpected question. She blushed with embarrassment as her friends stared at her, waiting for an answer. "Well, um, well, you see, I was, well, we were, um, well, planning on doing something else this weekend. Like, tomorrow, perhaps."

"I think it is a good idea to spend some quality time with him" said Laura. "It makes no sense to marry someone and not want to spend any time with them." The others nodded in agreement.

Ann's heart sank as Laura's words rang true. "Yes" she muttered, "that just doesn't seem right. But I promised him I would make it up to him for tomorrow. I just did not want to disappoint you all by not coming here as we had planned."

The rest of the day went all right. But throughout the day, Ann's friends kept saying largely positive things about their own husbands. Ann had very little positive things she could say about Thad. It was not because there was nothing positive to say about him. It was because she was indifferent and un-grateful to all the countless positive things about him. As her girlfriends gushed over how much they loved their husbands, Ann was dreading that they would peer pressure her into doing the same thing. "Please don't ask, please don't ask, please don't ask!" she muttered.

But inevitably, they did ask her about what made Thad so likeable. For a moment, Ann wanted to be honest about her feelings towards Thad, but she was afraid of what her friends would say and think. To further make matters worse, Sally was the only one to have actually met Thad some years ago, and she found him very likeable and gentlemanly. Ann knew that Sally would never accept Ann's true feelings towards Thad. So Ann decided to lie about it all.

"Well, here's the thing about Thad. He is the best man I have ever met. Except, perhaps, apart from my father. And if he were to die tomorrow, I would be the saddest wife on earth. I cannot imagine life without him. He means the entire world to me." Then Ann paused, put her hands over her face, and started to shed crocodile tears. Her friends had fallen for her performance and began to offer handkerchiefs and consolations.

"I am so sorry" she sniffed, "but I just can't go on like this. I just want to spend more time with Thad, but he just does not have time for me. He is just to busy with his work, and I know he loves me with all his heart. But he just does not prioritize my needs as he should. And I love him so much. I don't want us to grow apart."

"Oh well now, don't get yourself all worked up" soothed Lisa, "I am pretty confident that someday, in some way, you two will make it all up to each other."

Laura chimed in, "You said that you both had something planned tomorrow. Sounds like it will all turn up ok for you all."

Ann sighed while still wiping her eyes. "Yes, I am pretty sure that it will." But she was very unhappy at getting to spend time with Thad. For the rest of the day, Ann and her girlfriends went all around the mall. When evening came, they parted. Ann slowly walked back to her car and drove back home, dreading to return to Thad. As she feared, Thad was back home. He was waiting patiently for Ann to return.

"Hi sweetheart!" he declared as he hugged her lovingly. Ann tepidly reciprocated that gesture. "Good to be back home with you" she replied half-heartedly. Later on the tow of them were in bed, getting ready to turn in for the night. "Ann?" asked Thad, "how did your day go?"

Ann sighed, "It was a great time I had with my friends."

"I am glad to know that you had great time" Thad smiled. "How did your day go?"

"It also went fine. I just watched tv and took a walk in the park. I got pretty bored of staying home all day. That was why I asked if we could do something fun together tomorrow. We haven't done anything like that in a long time. I was hoping that maybe tomorrow we could just do that."

"What exactly had you got in mind?" Ann yawned.

"Well, maybe we could go to the mall or the park."

"I just went to the mall today. Perhaps we could go to the park instead."

"I was just thinking about that. I haven't been to the park in a long time with you. I have always gone there all by myself for the past, oh I don't know, year, maybe year and a half. I have waited forever for us to have an opportunity to be out together. I know that you love to be with your friends. But I need to be with you. That is what marriage is."

Ann sighed. "You are so right, Thad. I feel selfish for putting my desires over your needs. I promised you this morning that I would make it all up to you tomorrow, and that is just what I plan on. We can hang tomorrow, if you are still interested."

"Oh, yes I am!" declared Thad enthusiastically, "I have been thinking about visiting the mall. I haven't been there in a long time and would like to see it soon. I thought about seeing what has changed since I've last been there. Perhaps you could be my tour guide" he laughed.

Ann chuckled. "Ok big boy, I'll come with you tomorrow." Thad soon fell asleep, but Ann was fuming with rage at Thad's request to go out with her. She had a hard time sleeping with her raging thoughts racing around in her mind.

"That no-good, workaholic, boring husband of mine just has to spend his spare time here of all places doesn't he?" she thought to herself as she lay in bed staring at the ceiling. "I know he is exhausted from all his work, but can't he do something else instead of keeping his lazy ass inside the house all day long, let alone two days in a row. He can't leave me alone. He has to keep sticking his ass where it doesn't belong. Can't he keep to himself for just one day and leave me alone? Urghh! I've got to find a way to get rid of him once and for all!"

The following day was Saturday. As planned, Ann and Thad visited the mall that Ann and her girlfriends had visited yesterday. The mall was just about as busy and noisy as the previous day. Thad did not mind all the bustle, even though he was not used to too much noise. But he was so glad to be out with his wife that he did not seem to care for the noise.

"I haven't been to the mall in ages" he told Ann when they sat down at a bench. "I stopped going there a long time ago because I found it boring. The shops are all the same, although they do change every so often. Just about everything looks the same and seeing the same thing every day or even every week makes it less and less interesting. But the worst part about malls, is when there are sales events like Black Friday. Not only does it get more noisy, but it gets chaotic. I'm sure you have seen the stories online of people getting seriously hurt or even killed in these sales rushes, especially during the holidays. And what is all this rioting for? Stuff that people really don't need but just have an urge to buy it to impress each other. It is days like this when nothing special is going on, that I would love to visit the mall more often."

"I feel the same way" Ann replied half-heartedly. "Oh my!" she thought, "he's an even bigger crybaby than I realized. He wants some peace and quiet in a shopping mall, and he doesn't want to get crushed to death by holiday shoppers. Who the hell thought it was a good idea for me to marry this loser crybaby? Oh that's right, my lovely parents. Well they are just as rotten as he is. They are the reason why my life has been in such a miserable state that it has always been since I married Thad. Someday, everyone will pay for wrecking my life!"

The couple then stopped in front of a large mall directory located just in front of the escalator. As Thad was laser-focused on the map, Ann had an idea. "I can end my miserable marriage now and forever" she thought as she placed her hands on Thad's back so that she could push him down the escalator to his death. "Ann darling!" exclaimed a familiar voice. Thad and Ann turned around. It was Sally. "Oh my goodness, I wasn't expecting to see you back here so soon" she said she hugged Ann. "And is this your lovely hubby Thad?"

"O, no" Ann thought, "just when I had my perfect plan going, this bitch ruins it." But Ann quickly put on a fake smile while reciprocating the hug. "Sally! I was not expecting you here either."

"Oh, well coincidences like these happen! And you must be Thad!" she said turning towards the man and shaking his hand.

"Yes" Thad replied as he reciprocated the handshake, much to Ann's growing dismay.

"Oh, y-yes-s" stammered Ann, "This is my lovely hubby Thad. I am so glad that you could finally meet him."

Sally stared at Thad with a large grin. She looked all over him, especially in his eyes. She turned red in the face with the excitement of a fangirl.

"Ann has told me a lot about you over the years" said Sally as she placed her hands on his arms. "And she has told me all about what a fine young man you have been in all the years you two have been married. Well, maybe not young anymore, but you still have that thing in you that shows how much you love your bride even after all these years. She has told me nothing but the best about you. How you swept her off her feet when she was still young, and how you helped her find a good place to stay and be an anchor in her life all these years. I have never been married, or even been in love, but I want someone just like you some day."

"Well, Sally, I think you should keep on looking. Someday he will be there for you, even if it takes a while."

"Sure thing, Thad. And I hope I can have all the time that I can to spend quality time with him, as you and Ann are. You know, yesterday, Ann and I were hanging out together with our friends. And Ann started crying because she was unable to get any time with you, and she loved you so very much. I am so glad that you two are finally able to go out together."

Ann was cringing at this, because deep in her heart, she really did not want to spend any time with Thad. She was doing all this against her will and her better judgement. She also wanted to be honest with Thad some time in the near future, but Sally spilling the beans on Ann's fake tears was making Thad even more wanting to spend time with her.

Ann smiled as she watched and listened to the rest of their conversation. But privately she was getting angrier by the second as Sally was gushing over Thad. "Some friend I have" she thought to herself. "I have been her friend for years, and now when she meets Thad for the first time, she is much happier to see him than me. I can't believe that she would love him more than me."

Soon Sally was on her way, leaving Thad and Ann to resume their trip. "Looks like you have an interesting friend" he said as they walked around.

"I couldn't agree more" said Ann laughing nervously, though Thad thought she was laughing out of delight. "She certainly is the type of friend who makes everyone feel good. She makes strangers feel like longtime friends. I knew she was a sweet person when I first met her all those years back. I guess you could say that I am a good judge of character."

"Well, you certainly are. Just look at whom you married for example."

Ann tried to suppress her fake smile from turning into a frown. "Yes" she muttered, "it certainly shows."

After spending several more minutes at the mall, Thad wanted to leave and go some other place. "Would you like to try the Minnehaha Park?" he suggested to Ann. "I have been there several times, but I haven't been with you there in a long time. I think it would be good for us to enjoy some of mother nature for some time. It is right after noon now, so there is still some daylight left."

"Yes" said Ann half-heartedly, "I think we should make use of what is left."

Minutes later, they arrived at the park. It was quite crowded, as was expected on a weekend. The couple walked around, observing the sights such as the children playing sports, people walking their dogs, and the birds singing. Thad was happy to be here, but Ann was getting more and more agitated as she was desperately looking for ways to get rid of Thad. "I hope I can get rid of him soon today" she thought as they walked along, "and this time no one should interfere with my perfect plans, whatever they are."

As they continued to walk along the park, and while Ann was still forming her plans, Thad stooped and began to look at the Minnehaha Falls. "I have always loved going close to that waterfall" he said delightfully, "I never get tire of looking at it or photographing it. Let's get a closer look at it, shall we?"

Ann agreed to, and soon they walked towards the falls. As they got closer, Thad took out his phone to capture pictures.

As he stood at the edge of the creek to take pictures, Ann came up with an idea. She started to place her hands on his back in order to push him into the lake and drown him. "Motherfucker can't swim" she thought with excitement.

"Ann! Hello!" called out a familiar voice. Thad and Ann turned around. It was Lisa. She was out walking her bull terrier and had seen the couple. When Lisa saw Ann put her hands on Thad's back, she had assumed that Ann was about to give Thad a hug while he was taking pictures.

Ann took her hands off of Thad, and slowly walked over to Lisa and give her a weak hug, though Lisa compensated it by giving Ann a bear hug. "Oh Ann, it was so nice to see again this weekend! Sally just texted me that she met you and Thad at the mall today. What a coincidence that you two would end up here today as well! And how is Thad darling?" she said as she bear-hugged him as well. "I haven't seen you in a long time. Sally said she was so glad to finally meet you today. I hope everything is going along just fine for you!"

"Yes, things are certainly going on just fine since I last saw you" said Thad as he gave Ann and Sally a side hug. "I just have not been able to spend quality time with my baby in a long time. But now, we are lucky to have seized this opportunity to go out on a fantastic day like this. I just hope that more days like this are ahead of us."

"I am hoping for just the same" said Ann insincerely. "I have been unable to get such an opportunity like this forever, and it just so happened that today of all days was just that."

"Well I am glad to know that" said Lisa, "especially since Ann was sobbing yesterday over not having to spend time with you."

Ann once again cringed, though she hid this behind her smile. Sally continued, "But I am so glad you both finally got this opportunity for yourselves. Then she turned to look at her dog. "Oh! It looks like Benroy wants to go away. He hates loud noises, like the waterfall. It was good to see you two again, I look forwards to our next opportunity to visit!"

With that, Lisa and Benroy went away, leaving Thad and Ann together again. Thad sighed, "It looks like you really do have good judgement of character."

Ann also sighed, "Well, like I said, I certainly do have it."

They finished walking around the park before heading back home. Ann could not stop fuming to herself over just how her friends had unwittingly foiled her attempts at killing her husband. Thad, on the other hand, felt happy to spend the day with Ann. "I understand you wanting to spend more time with me" he said as he drove home, "and I know you have been waiting forever for this opportunity. But don't feel bad if we can't spend more time together. Things like this happen. But I think we should make time on our schedules for more days like this."

"Yes" muttered Ann, "I completely agree. I just could not control my emotions yesterday. But I am so glad we were able to finally get a chance."

That night, Thad was fast asleep, having cherished the fun day he just had. Ann was on the other end of the emotional spectrum. She could not fall asleep and rolling over in bed constantly over her rage and frustration over how the day went.

"What a ruined day this has been! I take this crybaby out to places that he has been begging me to like a spoiled child. I humored him all day, just to appease him so that he will never again pester me to mother him and take him out to places again. He seems fine with the way things went, but I wish I did not have to deal with such a guy like that. And to make matters worse, I had two perfect opportunities to get rid of him once and for all, and both times my friends just had to come over and ruin those chances just when I had it all going perfectly. And to add insult to injury, they tell Thad about my crying yesterday. I only put on that act so that those bitches would not think of me as strange if I told them I hated Thad. But now they have used it to make Thad want to spend even more time with me. As if spending a little time with that man baby was not miserably embarrassing enough. It sucks that I had just two aborted chances today to kill Thad. From now on, I need to get rid of him quickly and efficiently. I will make sure that no one stands in my way. And if they do, I will make them pay for this with their own lives."

The next day was Monday. Thad and Ann were preparing to return to their jobs. Thad was normally the first to be leaving the house, and Ann would leave about an hour later. That morning, as Thad was about to leave, he spoke to Ann. "I really enjoyed our time we spent over the weekend. I know that we don't get those opportunities that often. But if there is anything you need for me to do, I will be glad to help out my sweetheart."

With a hug and kiss, Thad went to his car and drove away. Ann stared at him through the widow until he drove away. "That son of a bitch wants to do anything for his sweetheart does he? I know exactly what he can do. Drop dead! That's all he's good for! That good for nothing bastard! The sooner he is dead and gone, the better my life will be!"

Before long, Ann had arrived to her job at the hotel. Within minutes after she began her work, she saw a familiar-looking man approach the front desk. "Good morning Mr. Denna! How was your weekend stay here?"

"Oh! It was fantastic! I have never been to the Twin Cities before, and I must admit, I was not disappointed by my visit Minneapolis! And now I must head over to St. Paul. I can't wait to see what that city has in store for me!"

"I am so glad that you had a great time here! I hope you come back again some time."

"Will try!" he said as he handed the key back to Ann. After checking him out, Ann watched him exit the hotel and get into his car. She sighed as her smile faded into a frown. "Good riddance to that nasty son of a bitch!" she hissed after making sure no one else was within earshot of her. "After what I had to endure yesterday, the last thing I need is more communication with more men!"

The rest of the day went on as usual. No prominent guests checked in or out on that day. She met her friends at work, who all shared what they had done over the weekend. For her part, Ann refused to talk about the previous day's engagement with Thad. Throughout the day, whether commuting to and from work, while on break, or on lunch, Ann's mind was constantly operating for ways to kill off Thad. But try as she might, she could not come up with feasible method.

CHAPTER 2

One day, when Ann was not working, she was sitting in her living room. Thad had been away for a few days, and Ann used this opportunity to invite over Emma, who was living in Chicago and was to be driving over. Ann kept staring at the window towards the driveway, and then to her phone to monitor for any messages or calls from Emma, as well as the time. Just before noon, an unfamiliar car with a familiar driver pulled into the driveway. Ann quickly walked out of the house just as Emma was getting out of the car. They embraced each other for several seconds, looked each other all over, and then walked into the house and sat in the living room.

"How has my baby sister been?" asked Ann.

"Oh, just fine. How have you been?"

"Same as always. How has your sports job been?"

"Well, it is getting better and better after every year. You know, sports journalism has long been a male-dominated field. Actually, sports and journalism are both male-dominated on their own, even now after all these decades.

"Does it ever get boring?" asked Ann with a little jealousy towards Emma.

"Well, let's just say that it is fairly routine when I have to be in the office all day long. Once I'm on an assignment, I get so happy to be able to visit a new place and be able to report on the major events such as the Super Bowl and other big playoffs. How about you? You deal primarily with just about the same people every day I understand. Does that ever get boring for you?"

"Yes, it does. Although in my case, I tend to deal with someone new just about every day. That only happens when a new guest checks in. But otherwise I still have to deal with the same bosses and coworkers. And now that I think of it, I don't ever remember seeing the same guest check in at different times. I guess you could say that excitement of seeing a new guest compensates for the monotony of dealing with the same people I work with."

"I see what you are getting at. Now tell me about Thad. How are things with him?"

Ann paused. She was quite hesitant about what to say next. "Well, things sure look ok for us. His job keeps him busy."

"Does he like his job?"

"Based on what he tells me, and how much he is devoted to it, you could very well say that he does like it very much. Between you and me, I think he likes his job more than he likes me."

"I don't know how you two manage, but if my husband spent loved his job more than me, I'd file for divorce. I can't understand why people get married and then spend much of their time isolated from each other. They are both better off single, just like me."

Ann bowed her head down in a moment of humility. She had to agree, even secretly, that Emma was very smart. "Well Emma, to be quite honest with you, I have considered filing for divorce from Mack many times."

Emma's eyes went bigger. "So the two of you have decided to call it quits?"

"I don't know what his plans are regarding our marriage. I doubt he plans on divorcing me. He seems to be in no hurry to call it quits as far as I'm concerned."

Emma was puzzled. "So you are planning on divorcing him, but you don't plan on telling him? Is that what you are getting at?"

Ann sighed. "Emma dear, I am sure you have heard the expression that absence makes the heart grow fonder. I guess who ever came with that was eager to see their loved one at their side at all times. And perhaps with some couples, they feel as though losing a partner, even for just a short period of time, is somehow akin to losing a part of themselves.

"But the longer I have been married to Thad, the more and more I cherish moments when he is absent. The longer he stays away from the house, the happier I feel. I feel free and happy, as I want to be. But whenever he comes back from his long journeys, I feel a sense of sadness and anger engulfing me. His mere presence irritates me to no end. Him constantly wanting to help me out in any way that he can, puts me at unease. In my experience, Emma, absence does not make the heart grow fonder. Instead, it makes the heart happier and more autonomous."

"But I thought you liked him very much. I remember at your wedding you said that you felt he was the love of your life and that he was just right for you then."

"That was then! This is now! Emma, darling, have you ever been in a romantic relationship with anyone at all?"

"No."

"Are you still trying to find the man of your dreams?"

"I'm not in any hurry, but if one should come, I would be so happy."

"Well, I have some news for you, since you are keeping the door open on having a relationship. When you are married, or in a romantic relationship of any kind, you need to basically walk on eggshells. There are certain things you cannot say, people you cannot see, places you cannot go to, things you cannot bring inside the house, and certain activities that you cannot engage in. That is because the person you are in a relationship with is constantly watching you. So if you step on even one small shell, you just as well might step on a landmine, because all it takes is one small misstep and the entire relationship is blown to smithereens.

"So when that other person is physically absent, at first you may feel lonely and sad. But after a while, you will soon come to appreciate these solitary moments. You will soon realize that there is value in not having someone look over your shoulder, even if it is someone you truly love. The more moments of isolation there are between the two of you, the more you will cherish the opportunity to not walk on eggshells anymore. Instead, you can tap dance all over the place and not have a care in the world, so long as your partner never finds out what you have been up to.

"Recently, Emma, I have been having a series of strange dreams that I think show the problems I am dealing with. In one dream, I get a call on my phone. I answer it. The voice on the other asks, 'Is this Mrs. Ann Noyd?'. I respond, 'Yes, this is she. How may I help you?'. The voice responds, 'Mrs. Noyd, I'm afraid I have some very bad news for you. It is regarding your husband, Thad.' 'What is it?' I ask. 'Well' says the voice, 'your husband has just been in a major, multi-vehicle accident on the highway. He has been taken to the nearest hospital and is fighting for his life. He may just still be alive at his moment. Just thought I would let you know'. I sigh. Then I reply, 'Thank you for letting me know', then I hang up. After I hang up, I start to feel a sense of joy and hope engulf my mind. I do not feel the slightest bit of sadness or shock, not even for a second. I feel so glad that Thad is lying in the hospital, edging towards death. I feel as though his incapacity is liberating for me, as I know that he will not be coming back home as soon as he had hoped he would. That gives me more autonomy to live my life the way I want to, even if that autonomy is brief.

"The second dream I have is when the phone rings, and I answer it. The voice on the other end says, 'Is this Mrs. Ann Noyd?'. 'Yes' I respond. 'Mrs. Noyd' says the voice, 'I am sorry to tell you this, but your husband Thad has been in a plane crash. He was taken to the nearest hospital. The doctors did everything that they could to save him, but I am sorry to say that they have failed. I am sorry for your loss'. I start to cry. The voice on the other end tries to comfort me but fails. Eventually, I hang up. As soon as I hang up, I feel as though a mask has fallen off my face. I feel free to express my true feelings. I suddenly realize that those tears I shed are just nothing but crocodile tears. I don't really feel sad that Thad has just died. I feel rejoiced and relieved that he has left his earth so abruptly. Many people, when a loved one has passed, feel as though their death brings about lost opportunities for things like enjoying life, or apologizing for some past bad behaviors. But I don't feel sad at all at his passing. I feel as though his death is an opportunity in and of itself, all by itself. Instead of crying, I feel like breaking into a dance and song to celebrate my freedom. I feel like a caged bird that has just been suddenly released. No more walking on eggshells. From now on, I can tap dance myself to a happy life that I deserve!"

"Are you saying that you are unhappy with being married to Thad?" asked Emma, still perplexed.

"Absolutely!"

"So, are you going to divorce him them?" asked Emma, slightly exasperated by Ann's confusing statements.

"No!" replied Ann assertively.

"So the two of you have decided to reconcile and resolve your problems and remain married then."

"No, nothing of that sort."

Emma was getting more and more perplexed and frustrated. "So if you both are not divorcing, and you're not resolving your issues, then what are you both planning on?"

Ann smiled. "It is not *we*, Emma dear, it is only *I*. I, and I alone, have decided what course of action to take regarding my marriage and my life! And I have decided that it would be better for me to have Thad dead."

Emma gasped, "Y-you w-want him dead?"

"Yes!" declared Ann, "a dead husband is better than a boring, useless husband!"

"Boring?! Useless?! How is he these things? I thought you told me that he was the greatest guy you could have tied the knot with!"

"All he does is. He also pays the bills, does the yard work, and other mundane things. He is too much of a good guy. I want to have a bad guy for once as my husband, or even just as a boyfriend."

Emma paused to regain her thoughts. "Oh!" she gasped, "you mean like those James Dean or Marlon Brando types!"

"NO!" screamed Ann, "those guys are pussies. I want really bad guys, like Ted Bundy, Ted Kaczynski or Clyde Barrow. Those guys know just how to be bad as hell. Thad is too much of a gentleman."

Emma began to laugh nervously. "You don't really want to fall in love with such horrible guys like, do you?"

"Oh yes I do! But I don't just want to fall in love with a bad boy. I want to be a bad girl. And to start things off, remember I said that Thad is better off dead because he is so boring and useless? Well, I have decided to have him killed and –"

"STOP!!" exclaimed Emma.

"Is there a problem?" asked Ann in a casual manner.

"A problem? Ann, you want to murder your own husband!"

Ann smiled. "Why, yes dear, that is my plan. And I want you to be a part of it."

Emma put her hands on her forehead. "No no no" she groaned, "I can't believe that my own sister would want to shed innocent blood!"

"Thad may be innocent, but he is too innocent and boring for his own good."

Emma began to cry. "Why can't you just divorce him? You will save yourself a lot of trouble!"

"Emma dear, there is no fun in going to court to end a marriage. Besides, shedding some blood is way more fun and will put a quick end to all my problems. Remember, no pain means no gain!"

"No it won't!" screamed Emma as she bolted towards the front door. But no sooner had she placed her hand on the doorknob than Ann slapped it off and stood between her and door.

"So you want to leave so soon, little sissy? Fine! Leave! But before you go, I have some words of wisdom for you. This will come in handy once you are older. One day, you will come across a man. Maybe you've seen him before, maybe you haven't. Perhaps you know him quite well, or he's just someone you had a casual acquaintance with. But soon after you meet him, you start to fall in love with him. And he also falls in love with you. Pretty soon, you both desire each other's presence more and more.

"Then one fine day, he will propose to you in some memorable fashion. And you will be overcome with joy. And you will accept his proposal. Shortly after, you are both married in a grand wedding ceremony. And you feel like you have just been on top of the world. And he feels like he has finally got the girl of his dreams, while you feel like you have finally got the man of your dreams.

"After all the glamorous celebrations, you will soon settle into your new normal life. It may get some adjusting to for the both of you, but soon you will get the hang of it. And soon, you will go about on your new daily activities without making any second thoughts about all of it. You may or may not have kids, depending what you two can plan on, but that is irrelevant to the bigger scheme of things.

"A few years pass. They will pass much faster than you can keep track of. When you finally find out how much time has indeed passed, you are in for a shock. And you wonder how you never realized this much sooner. And soon you try to make sense of it all. And you decide what to do with your life now. Something meaningful. It is then that you realize that the man of your dreams, whom you have spent the past number of years with, is now a total stranger. And you don't know him. And before long, you don't want to know him because you used to know everything about him. The man whom you once loved and felt like you never could live without, is now someone whom you want to get away from because he is no longer glamorous. He is now just average and boring. He is stranger who keeps looking over your shoulder, causing you to walk on eggshells and limit your activities.

"It is at that moment that you realize, that the one person in the entire world, who cares even remotely about you, is you loving, caring, older sister. And you want to run to her as she keeps her arms open to you. But then you realize that big sister cannot help. Big sister was having a problem many years ago and asked for your help. But back then, little sister did not want to help big sister, because you were a selfish coward. You didn't even try to help get your sweet, older sister out of her problem, so big sister will not help you now."

Emma pushed Ann out of the way, opened the door, and ran straight to her car. As she drove away, Ann stared at her through the open door. "Just you wait, you little selfish bitch" she muttered, "just you wait."

CHAPTER 3

A few days had gone by. Ann was back at her job. When her shift was over, she headed back to her car. On her way to the car, she looked at her phone and noticed a voicemail had been left by Emma. "Hi, Ann. I was, um, thinking about our conversation a few days back when I visited you. And I have given it a lot of thought and have decided to go along with your plan to murder Thad after. So, whenever you can, please call me back and let me know what your plans are."

For a split second, Ann thought it very strange that Emma would suddenly make a reversal on agreeing to the plot against Thad. But soon, Ann was so overjoyed by her sister's change of heart that she completely forgot to even think of asking her that. Immediately after getting into her car, Ann called Emma.

"Hi Emma, dear! I just got your message. I knew that you would eventually see the light and come to your senses."

"Well, I sure did. Now how do you plan on killing Thad?"

"Well, I prefer him to die in a violent bloody manner."

"What exactly do you have in mind, Ann?"

"Anything that brings about bloodshed and unbearable pain onto him. Traffic accident. Gun shot to the head. Beaten to death by a street gang. Lynched by an angry mob. Attacked by wild animals. Trapped in a burning building. Burnt at the stake. You name it. The bloodier and more painful, the better!"

"That sounds pretty interesting. But have got a specific type of plan in mind?"

"Well, yes I have. If this plan works out the way it should, nobody will have a reason to suspect us even in the slightest. Now here's how it goes. Thad is supposed to return home next week from some financial conference in Indianapolis. After he arrives, he will be fast asleep, since he is a heavy sleeper. While he is asleep, we will both stab him to death. Then we will take his body, put it in the trunk of my car, drive to a rundown part the inner city, and dump his body on the street. The police will assume that some of the animals who live in the ghettos have kidnapped, tortured, and murdered him."

"Just a second", interrupted Emma, "but what exactly do you mean by 'animals who live in the ghettos?'"

"Niggas!", exclaimed Ann.

There was a pause on the other end of the call. "Oh", Emma finally said, "I understand."

"Yes indeed!" said Ann, "while the police are busy profiling and invading the black communities for the suspects, we will get away with it scot-free. Assuming of course that there are no hiccups in my brilliant plan! So what do you think, little sister? Shall we proceed with it?"

Emma sighed faintly. "Yes, I think that we should."

"Good then! Now Thad is set to return next Tuesday. Be sure to check yourself into a nearby hotel no later than Monday. Tuesday night be on alert for a text from me. As you as you receive it, come straight over. I will give you more instructions when you arrive." With that, the two of them hung up on each other and went their separate ways. Ann drove back home feeling high and mighty about herself.

The following Tuesday arrived. Ann had arrived back to her house from her job during the night. She saw Thad's car on the driveway. "Well", she said to herself, "he sure is here a little earlier than I had expected. But he's here nonetheless!"

She went slowly into the house. Most of the lights inside had been turned off. Ann tiptoed upstairs to the bedroom. The door was closed, so she opened it very slowly. The room was dark. Ann saw Thad sleeping on one side of the bed. "Perfect" she thought to herself, and slowly closed the door. Ann texted Emma as planned. Minutes later, Emma pulled into the driveway and slowly made her way to the hallway just outside the bedroom. Ann had left the front door slightly open for Emma to make a quick entry. Ann was standing in the hallway with a long, large knife she had purchased a few days earlier for this night.

"Now here is the plan", she whispered, "we will both go inside. You pull back the sheet, while I stab him. Then we will wrap his body in the sheets and take him into his car and dump him as planned."

They both walked into the room with their shoes off to not make any sound. They both went on either side of the bed. When Ann gave the signal, Emma turned on the lamp and quickly pulled back the sheet. Ann was about to stab Thad. But it was not Thad, it was a policeman! He pointed his gun into Ann's face and yelled "Freeze!!"

Ann dropped the knife and headed for the doorway. Two officers immediately emerged, one from the bedroom closet and another from the hallway. They both grabbed Ann's arms and handcuffed her before pressing her against the wall. The officer who had been lying in bed stood.

"Mrs. Ann Noyd!" he barked, "you are under the arrest for conspiring to murder your husband!" As he read the Miranda rights, Ann looked over to Emma, who was crying. "Do you understand these rights as I have explained them to you?" asked the officer. "Yes" replied Ann. "Do you wish to waive your right to remain silent?" Ann looked over to Emma. "No!" she screamed, "and fuck that bitch!" as she lurched forward to try and kick her sister. The officers fastened their grasp on her before dragging her out to the police car that had just arrived.

Upon arriving at the nearest station, Ann was booked on the charge and placed in an interrogation room. Several of the officers present during her arrest planned to interrogate her. "Emma ratted to you about my plan, right?" she asked the officers icily.

"Not only did she rat us about your plan", one officer replied, "but she also agreed to have her phone tapped to listen in on your conversation last week about killing your husband. It was our department that urged her to call you and pretend to change her mind about going along with your plan. Not only were we recording that conversation, we also had a camera inside the master bedroom in your house that recorded everything you said and planned on doing."

"Where is Thad?" she asked angrily.

"Somewhere that you will not know. We reached out to him and told him about your plan and played your phone conversation with your sister. We told him to not go back to his house. Instead, he left his car at our station where our men took it to your house to use it as bait to catch."

CHAPTER 4

The day finally arrived when Ann appeared before the Honorable Judge Warren Peese for her bail hearing. Ann's attorney was Amy G. Dala, one of the most prominent criminal attorneys in Minnesota.

The prosecutor, Garland Springley, beseeched the court into keeping Ann behind bars in while awaiting trial. "Your Honor, the defendant clearly poses a serious threat towards her potential victim. She has shown no signs of remorse for her actions and has repeatedly displayed antisocial behavior while incarcerated. She has violated four restraining orders placed and two court orders against her by using the jail phone to leave profanity-laced voicemails against both of her parents, as well as her sister and estranged husband. She is not be let out at all until trial commences."

"Your Honor" said Dala, "my client is suffering from immense emotional distress from having to be locked up for a crime she did not commit. She is afraid that someone dangerous will attack during the night while she is asleep, or with her back turned towards the aggressor. The defendant is currently going through a divorce hearing and is better off being released with an ankle monitor until the trial commences."

Judge Peese listened to the arguments posed by the prosecution and the defense. He then made his decision. "The court finds by clear and convincing evidence that the defendant poses a danger to the safety of the allegedly intended victim and the community, particularly in light of the serious risk that the defendant would commit witness intimidation, as evidenced by her alleged conduct in attempting to assault a witness during her arrest and her disobedience of court orders while in custody. The defendant has expressed a lack of impulsive control both during her arrest, and while in custody. This court therefore denies the defendant any bail."

"Well Ann" said Dala as they were escorted out of the courtroom by officers, "I warned you not to disobey those orders. Not only have you forfeited any possibility of getting bailed out, if anyone would be willing to in the first place, but you also have given the prosecution a good argument for keeping you behind bars for good."

Ann did not answer. She simply glared at her attorney as the cops escorted her back to jail. A few days later, Dala met Ann in the jail to discuss the upcoming trial. "Now listen very carefully to me Ann. The trial is set to commence in 4 months. Now we need to try and give ourselves the best argument we can come up with before the first trial. It is no doubt going to be very hard, considering that the prosecution has a lot on you that could get you a guilty verdict at the drop of a hat. And your behavior since your incarceration isn't helping much at this time.

"Now, here is one thing we can do to get you a light sentence. I think it would be better for you to change your plea deal from not guilty to guilty. Like I said, the evidence against you is overwhelming, and trying to get the prosecution to prove your guilt with you pleading not guilty will open up a can of worms. Are you willing to change your plea?"

"No!" said Ann, "I will not give them a chance to make me look like a bad person!"

"They are already doing just that. And the judge does not seem to be any less sympathetic to you. Perhaps admitting to your guilt will get a lighter sentence."

Ann thought about it. "Plead guilty?" she thought to herself, "and admit to being the evil person that they want to portray me as? I will not give them that chance! I will not go down without a fight!" Her ego simply could not tolerate admitting to guilt despite irrefutable evidence.

Dala sighed, "You are setting yourself up for failure! Do you realize that by coming clean in the court, you actually may have a decent chance of spending less time behind bars?"

"Getting me to spend little or no time behind bars is your task!" retorted Ann.

Dala sighed with frustration. "Ann, please, I'm trying to help you. You entered a not guilty plea, so you are forcing the prosecution to lay out all the facts they have against you. Now if you enter a guilty plea, then the prosecution will not have to lay out all these facts, and they might even recommend the court to give you a lighter sentence."

"If the prosecution wants to drag my name though the mud, then we'll give them a ride for their money!"

"Fine then! Since you will not go with the easy way, we will have two much harder ways. One way is to shop around for a female judge. Studies have shown that, on average, female judges are more lenient towards defendants in terms of sentencing, especially if the defendant is also a woman. Now the good news is that I have been able to find a female judge in this jurisdiction. The bad news is, she is set to officially retire less than a week from now. It's anyone's guess as to whether her replacement is also a woman. Hopefully, it will be one. But I cannot guarantee it.

"A second more feasible method we could go for is to request a jury trial. A typical jury consists of 12 members. We could try to get a majority of them female. That would give us a slightly better chance of getting acquitted, since studies have shown that female-majority juries also tend to be more lenient towards female defendants. Either way, even if we get a conviction, we could still get a lighter sentence."

"I don't want a light sentence" said Ann, "I want to be acquitted. I deserve to be free to live my life the way I see fit. No judge or jury, man or woman, is going to ever get in my way the way Thad did!"

Dala rolled her eyes and frowned. "You need to carefully guard what you say in public" she chastised Ann. "Statements like that, when made in public or in the company of interrogators, will be used against you in court. It won't help you win at all."

About a week before the trial was to begin, Dala and Ann met to go over their plans. "I have good news and bad news for you" said Dala.

Ann smiled. "Oh please give me the good news! I have been waiting for an eternity to hear such things!"

"Very well then. First off, I managed to get us a mostly-female jury. I'm sure you'll find that 10 out of 12 is quite extraordinary."

"It is just what we need!" said Ann delightfully, "but now how on earth did you get so many women jurors?"

"Simple. I used peremptory challenges to remove as many male candidates as I could. Of course, in order to throw suspicion off of myself, I decided to select a couple of male jurors."

"Well, that is really great! But now, what is the bad news?"

"Well, I was unable to get us a female judge. The one judge who was on the bench and retired just after your bail hearing was replaced by a man. The judge we are about to go against is a veteran who is notorious for his harsh sentences on violent criminals. even those who have been charged merely with attempted acts of violence, such as murder or kidnapping, don't have a prayer when in the courtroom of Warren Peese. I guess we have to brace ourselves for a heavy sentence."

"What do you mean 'we'?" asked Ann angrily.

Dala was perplexed. "The two of us. I am still going to be defending you."

"Not anymore!"

Dala gasped. "What on earth are you talking about?"

"I am talking about me firing you from representing me, bitch!"

"But why would you do such a thing? I managed to get us a female-dominated jury. And my track record has been pretty good."

"The hell with your track record! I am sacking you because you did not get me female judge as you promised!"

"First of all, I never promised you a female judge. I said that there may be a possibility of us getting a female judge. That is hardly a promise."

"Promise or no promise, I wanted a female judge and you spent the past few months doing nothing about it!

"There was nothing I could do. There are no female judges in this jurisdiction. I had no choice Ann. Beggars cannot be choosers."

"I am not interested in your pathetic excuses! I wanted a female judge, you don't give me one, so the hell with you, bitch!"

"All right, fine. But who is going to defend you in court?"

"I will!"

"Are you sure you can adequately represent yourself in court against the charge of attempted murder?"

"Yes."

"And what makes you so confident?"

"Because I can. I want this opportunity to show that judge and prosecutor who's boss!"

"I am warning you, Ann, that you are setting yourself up for a large defeat. You have no legal experience. You don't know the law or the court procedures as well as I do. You need someone with a thorough knowledge of our justice system on your team."

"I don't nee to know all of that legal garbage. I just want an opportunity to face those sons of bitches and show them who's boss!"

"You can't win this way Ann! Bluffing your way through a trial almost never succeeds."

"Yes I can! You are just jealous of me because you cannot charge me for your services anymore. Now fuck off, bitchy!"

The first day of the trial commenced. Springley the prosecutor gave the opening statement. "Ladies and gentlemen of the court. The defendant, Miss Ann Noyd, is a cold-hearted, bloodthirsty, psychopath who wanted her then-husband, Thaddeus Penter, dead because she wanted to live her life as a criminal, and she felt that he would be a good person to start with. The defendant attempted to solicit assistance from her sister Emma, who promptly refused and instead went to the police, where she had agreed to have her cell phone conversations with the defendant recorded, as well as setting up a trap to catch the defendant in the act of attempting to murder her husband. During the recorded conversations, and in the aftermath of her arrest and detention, Miss Noyd has not shown the slightest bit of remorse for her actions. She has instead, while awaiting for her trial, engaged in antisocial behavior towards other people, such as her ex-husband, her sister Emma, and her parents by disobeying court orders and restraining orders and placing calls to these people. In ever one of these instances, she has left profanity-ridden voicemails.

In light of these things, the prosecution calls for the jury to sentence the defendant to the maximum penalty of 12 years in prison."

Ann then stood up to make her opening remarks. She was wearing a business suit. "Members of the jury. This case against me is nothing more than a sexist witch hunt. The prosecutor is a man. The judge is a man. Clearly, there is misogyny involved in this. Neither the judge nor the prosecutor would ever do a thing like this to a man. This cell phone recording between me and my sister was just a friendly chat among sisters. The video of my arrest was a setup for a reality tv show. It was all just a joke that has been misconstrued by sexist men into something that it is not. I will not let this sexist case go away without a fight. I will not let the sexist prosecutor get away with his joke of a case. And I hope that you great people in the jury will be smart enough to see through all the misogyny that I am enduring, and will find me innocent, because that is what I am. And I intend to prove my innocence, or die trying."

The prosecution called for its first witness, Officer Sam Bexler, whom Emma had gone to in order to report Ann's murder plans. "Officer Bexler" said Springely, "will you tell the court what happened on the day that Ms. Emma Noyd came to your station?"

"Certainly. This woman, Emma, came to our front desk, and told the desk duty officer that her sister Ann was planning on murdering a Mr. Thaddeus Penter, the husband of Ann, and had asked Emma's help in carrying out the alleged plan."

"Objection!" shouted Ann.

"What are you talking about?" asked Judge Peese.

"I object to the slanderous way this officer is portraying me! What he has just said is absolutely false, and I want him to stop this gossiping about me!"

"Ms. Noyd, you are out of order. I guess since you have fired your attorney and chosen to represent yourself, you did not have time to go over the legal procedures. You cannot object to a witness' testimony. You can only object to a prosecution's line of questioning. Now don't you ever again interrupt a witness how is giving testimony, or else I will have to throw you out of this courtroom for contempt of court. The witness may continue."

"Emma told us about what Ann had told her earlier that day. We came to the decision to have Emma call Ann about a week from now and pretend that she had changed her mind about murdering Mr. Penter. Emma had also agreed to have her phone conversations with the defendant recorded."

"Now will you tell the court how you managed to set up the defendant's arrest?"

"Objection!" shouted Ann with a large smile.

"On what grounds?" sighed the judge.

"On the grounds that the question is full of gossip and innuendo."

"Objection overruled! Witness may proceed to answer question."

"Thank you, Your Honor. After we made the recording, we approached the alleged target while he was out of town, and showed him the recordings. We asked that he allow us to put him under witness protection, and permission to use his car that he left at the airport in Minneapolis as a trap for the defendant."

After Springley had cross-examined him, Ann took her turn. "Officer Bexler. My sister Emma came to you on that day and told you that I had planned on killing my husband, am I right?"

"That is correct."

"Did she give a reason as to why I would want my husband dead?"

"She said that you wanted to live a criminal lifestyle. And that you were getting bored of living with him."

"Did you have any reason to believe that my sister was telling you the truth?"

"Yes I did."

"And what reason was that?"

"Because our policy in the force is to take allegations like this seriously until the facts prove otherwise."

"So you had Emma's permission to secretly record out phone conversation. Is that correct?"

"It is correct."

"And did you have my permission to record our conversations?"

"Objection!" said Springley, "That line of questioning is not relevant."

"Sustained!" ruled Judge Peese.

"So what did you guys do after my sister spoke to you?"

"After she agreed to let us tap her phone, she agreed to call you and tell you that she had changed her mind and now had wanted to go along with your plans."

"So you told her to trick me into thinking that she had changed her mind after all. Is that right?"

"It is right, yes."

"So you were hiding in my house when I came back on that day. How did you get inside my house?"

"Emma let us in."

"So what you are saying is that you guys, along with Emma, burgled my house in order to arrest me, is that right?"

"Objection!" said Springley. "Defense is leading the witness."

"Sustained" ruled Judge Peese.

"No further questions."

"The prosecution wishes to call upon Emma Noyd." The witness came forth and was sworn to tell the truth. She then proceeded to explain everything that had happened since that day she visited Ann, from Ann's plan to murder Thad to the obscene voicemail Ann had left her. It then came time for Ann to cross-examine her. Emma was terrified at having to face her sister and speak with her directly for the first time in months, in light of all that had unfolded.

"Ms. Noyd" began Ann sarcastically, "did you agree to have your phone conversations recorded?"

"Yes."

"Now did you agree to record only the conversations just between you and me, or was it for all of your phone calls?"

"It was for only the ones between me and you."

"Now, then, you told the court that you are ashamed of me, and that you cannot believe that someone like me would be so terrible. Tell me now, do I look like a terrible person to you?"

Before Springley could object, Emma started crying "Yes! That is just what you are!"

For the duration of the trial, Springley brought forth some of Ann's girlfriends who had often heard her talk about her desire to become a criminal and kill Thad. When Ann cross-examined them, she tried to question their sanity or sobriety. "Your Honor, I think it is clear that all this talk about me wanting be a criminal is all hearsay. These women all claim to have heard me make these statements while I was drunk. But surely, they themselves could have also been drunk as well during those instances."

The day came for both parties to make their closing statements. Springley was the first to do so. "Ladies and gentlemen of the jury. I have said it before, and I will say it again. The defendant, Ann Noyd, is a heartless psychopath who should not be allowed to roam around free on the face of this earth. She has a strong desire to live a criminal lifestyle, and has shown no remorse for her actions. She has proven herself to be a danger towards those whom she has a vendetta on, and has recklessly disobeyed legal orders. The prosecution strongly believes that not only is the defendant to be found guilty, but she is to be given the maximum penalty as prescribed by the law of 12 years incarceration, without any possibility of parole."

Then it was Ann's turn to make her own closing arguments to the jury. "Ladies and gentlemen. As I have said before, I am innocent of this charge that the prosecution has brought upon me. I think you will all find it very obvious that this is the result of a misogynistic prosecutor who just wants to persecute me because I am a woman. If I were a man, he would not have brought this case against me and drag me through all this mud. I also think it is clear how rigged this trial is that the judge, who is also a man, as always overruled my objections, but has never once overruled Mr. Springley's objections. I urge you all to look at me for who I really am. I am an innocent woman who has endured lots of sexism all of my life. And I deserve to have my chance to be heard and be released from all this pain that I have had to endure these past few months, let alone my entire life. Do not let this witch hunt against me win out."

The jury then went away to deliberate. They returned in less than half an hour. "Members of the jury" declared Judge Peese, "have you reached a verdict?"

The jury foreman stood up to read the verdict. "Yes we have, Your Honor. We the jury find the defendant, Hannah Bell Noyd, guilty on one count of attempted murder against one Thaddeus Penter."

Ann quickly flew into a rage. "You bitches!!" she screamed, "How could you do this to me! I told you not to let these sexist men persecute me any longer, and you betrayed me! You will pay for this! We women need to stand together to fight sexism, and you bitches all betrayed me!! You will all pay for this some day!!"

As she was still ranting, the guards quickly grabbed hold her and dragged her out of the courtroom. The foreman continued reading, "We recommend the maximum penalty of 12 years incarceration as prescribed by law."

A few days later, Ann once again faced Judge Peese for her formal sentencing. This time, she and the judge were to square off together. "Ms. Ann Noyd" he began, "you have been found guilty by a jury your peers of attempted murder. The jury has recommended the maximum penalty of 12 years of incarceration. I have taken into consideration your recklessness, your disregard for the safety of your alleged victim and the witnesses. In my many years on this bench, I have never seen a more evil woman than yourself. I am very certain that hell itself would not scorn you once you reached its gates. You not only have no remorse for your actions, but you also have the nerve to call yourself a victim of misogyny. You have not only disgraced yourself, but your entire family. Your ex-husband is scared for his life, even after you have been put behind bars. Your sister is traumatized by your evil, and both of your parents are dead because of you! And even now you still are unable to show any signs of emotional intelligence. You have shown no signs of regret over how this has affected you or your family for the worse, and only for the worse! I have decided to sentence you to the maximum penalty. Case closed!"

CHAPTER 5

Once Ann began her long sentence in an all-female prison, she tried her hardest to integrate into prison life. At first. She found it to be monotonous and boring. She would engage in the same routine every day, see the same inmates and guards, and wear the same color prison outfit. Soon she began to get used to her new life, primarily because it put her into limited contact with men, which was just what she wanted. "No men, no problems!" she would tell herself whenever she wanted to take her mind off her otherwise miserable prison life.

One day, about 2 years into her sentence, Ann went to see the warden. "Hello, Ann" said the warden, "now what is that you want to see me about?"

"It is regarding that male guard whom I keep seeing just about every day" replied Ann in an irritated manner.

"Has he done anything to you?"

"No. Except that he is a man, and he makes me feel uncomfortable, and I don't like having him poking his nose where he does not belong. I want him to be take away from this facility at once!"

The warden started laughing. "Well, Ann, considering what you got yourself into prison for in the first place, I am not surprised that you would hate men so much. Especially considering what an ungrateful little bitch you are!"

Ann wanted to tear his face apart. But she knew it would only land her in more trouble, as there was a guard standing just outside the office. "In the 9 years since I have taken over this prison" the warden continued, "I have had my fair share of really absurd requests from inmates. But yours very much reigns supremely stupid. Your request is denied, not the least bit on the grounds that banning men from working in this facility will land me in legal trouble with discrimination lawsuits. But if it is any comfort to you, I would like to put you in solitary confinement for the rest of your sentence. That way you will not have to deal with any men, or women, for that matter. Now, do you prefer that, or will you get back there and learn to adapt and cooperate?"

Ann sighed. "On second thought" she muttered, "just forget my request."

The warden chuckled. "Easier said than done! But I'll try."

Ann soon left the office fuming profusely. "I hate having that son of a bitch wandering around like a wild animal. He makes me uncomfortable. He has ruined the one thing that I like about being in prison. I will not let him get away from this. If the warden will not get rid of that male guard, then I will, somehow!"

Before long, Ann began to devise her own plan to get rid of the male guard. She began a whisper campaign among the prisoners that the male guard had done something terrible to one of their fellow inmates. "He sexually assaulted a former inmate" she would tell some of her inmates, "that's why she got transferred out of here a while back."

Ann had only told this to a handful of the inmates, but like wildfire, this rumor spread to just about the entire facility population. But along the way, the rumor had taken several variations. "He beat her up". "He molested her". "He groped her." "He raped her". Before anyone could get the facts straight, this bad word-of-mouth had the entire population fuming and scheming for revenge. It did not matter what the male guard had been accused of. What mattered was that he had done something bad and needed to be punished in some way, especially a drastic one.

Eventually, almost all of them had secretly begun forming a plan. One night, the male guard was making his rounds on the top balcony. It was just hours before mandatory bedtime. Everything seemed quiet and in order, as it usually was the case. Suddenly, several inmates ambushed him from behind. They placed some blankets over his head, disarmed him, and then proceeded to tie him up using their belts. As they placed duct tape over his mouth, dozens of more inmates swarmed onto him like wolves. They pressed his back against the wall and started punching him in the face. Soon they began hitting him with a variety of blunt instruments such as pans, pots, glass bottles, and shoes.

The male guard's frantic screaming was muffled by the tape. Some of the inmates had managed to grab hold of some knives from the kitchen and were stabbing him repeatedly in the chest and stomach. He tried in vain to wrest himself out of their grip but could not. As he struggled to maintain his standing, his assailants used the knives to cut off his ears, nose, fingers, penis, and testicles. They were also disemboweling him. His muffled screaming grew louder and more desperate as his pain became more and more intense.

Finally, some of the assailants took a long string made from bedsheets. They tied one end around his neck, and the other onto the railing of the balcony. Then they all lifted him up and flung him over the railing. As the guard remained hanging and swinging around, his blood and internal organs rained down to the ground floor.

Very quickly, the facility was placed on lockdown and the armed guards swarmed around, sending tear gas against the rioters. In a matter of minutes, order was restored. The rioters were all rounded up and placed in whatever cells were available. The guard was set free and taken to the prison hospital where he was declared dead.

Immediately, the authorities began to investigate the instigators of the riot. They had a hard time, because no one really knew who had started the rumors against the male guard, nor could they pin down who had originally instigated the riot. As for Ann, she was largely able to avoid being implicated in the matter. During the incident, she was working the night kitchen detail with several other inmates. Ann had specifically volunteered for that night as she knew in advance what was about to happen. She wanted to take part in the riot, but very quickly decided against it. She knew that the prison was crammed with security cameras, and that her involvement would be promptly caught and that she would have been in a lot of trouble, the worst of it being sentenced to life in prison for the victim's murder. "The last thing I need is more of the same" she pondered.

The authorities questioned every prisoner, whether or not they had taken any part in the riot. Ann used this as an opportunity to get on their good side. She knew that they would be suspicious of her, since she had earlier asked the warden to remove the male guard from the premises. So Ann decided to throw her fellow inmates under the bus in order to throw the scent off of herself. Even the ones who had not participated in the incident in any way were not spared.

"I know who is responsible for this tragedy" she told the authorities. "And I also know why they did this. I cannot say I saw it coming, but I understand why they would do this. A number of them had told me that they were unhappy with the living conditions. Others told that their rights as prisoners were being routinely violated. But they all had something or the other to complain about. And they felt like their requests were not being met. And that made them upset.

"But none of them had ever told me anything about being violent towards anyone, let alone that poor guard. I am just as taken aback by this as anyone else is. I did not see this coming. But believe me, those women had an understandable motive for what they did. Those women are some of the nicest people I have ever met. At least, I thought they were until now. But I guess that they just had a lot of pent-up frustration and were yearning for a way to let it all out. It was very well just a cry for help."

Based on Ann's testimony, dozens of her fellow inmates were prosecuted and punished for the murder of the male guard. The ones who were caught on the security cameras physically assaulting and killing the guard were convicted of murder and sentenced to life in prison. But several who had not participated in the riot were instead punished through different means such as having their privileges revoked or being sent to solitary confinement. Most of them were innocent of the matter and pleaded their innocence to the authorities. But since Ann had been the most cooperative, the authorities took her word hook, line and sinker while ignoring the testimonies of the falsely accused inmates. Ann was given full immunity from prosecution in exchange for her cooperation with the authorities. In addition, she was also given several privileges by the prison staff.

Before long, the prison was back to normal. Except that now, there were more male guards than before and they were all heavily armed and trained to respond to unrest at the drop of a hat. "Just what I always wanted!" Ann grumbled to herself. "Those guys were supposed to have been intimidated and scamper off in fear for their own lives and safety. But now they have brought reinforcements and are now sticking their noses around even more and watching our every move, as if the hundreds of surveillance cameras are not bad enough! O well, might as well enjoy it while it lasts. At least I only have about 10 more years left."

Ann had tried to come up with ways to get rid of as many of the male guards as she could but was unable to come up with any feasible methods. She soon abandoned her plans and decided it was in her best interest to keep a low profile and get on the prison staff's good side. Ann decided to be a model prisoner, very friendly and very cooperative with the prison staff. She was never given any disciplinary points.

Early on during her incarceration, Ann would be honest to her fellow inmates about how she hated men, wanted to be a criminal, and why she wanted Thad dead. But they would all just laugh at her and give her the cold shoulder. It did not take long for Ann to realize that this was no way to make friends, as even the most psychopathic of the female inmates did not hold misandristic views.

So Ann devised a way to make them her friends instead of turning them against her. She would tell them that she wanted Thad dead because he was abusing her. "I was scared for my life" she would tell the inmates, "and I was desperately trying to escape my situation. No one would help me. No one could help me. I had no other family members to turn to. Divorce would have been long, costly, and ugly. I had no choice but to have killed off quickly. Of course, I got caught before I had my chance. But at least, it is all behind me now. We are now divorced, and Thad was able to hire a really good attorney to take away all of my personal belongings, as well as my assets.

But although he is still alive and roaming the face of this earth with my belongings, I am glad that I will probably never see him ever again, as long as either of us are still alive."

Ann's heartbreaking story, along with her crocodile tears, caused every inmate who heard her story to be sympathetic towards her. after all, many of them had been in bad relationships or come from bad families before going to prison. They tried their best to make her feel at home.

Ann, for her part, decided to also show sympathy towards inmates who came from abusive backgrounds. She wanted to dispel any idea that she was heartless and cruel, so she feigned empathy towards them. Whenever any of them would recount their tragic stories, Ann would break out into crocodile tears and embrace them to feign giving comfort to the distressed. It was through this modus operandi that Ann managed to avoid any suspicion from falling onto her during her incarceration.

CHAPTER 6

Within the next few days leading up to her release, Ann was required to sign some paperwork. On the day of her release, Ann was given all of her personal belongings back. this included her clothes, shoes, and cash. Ann's car was taken away and given to Thad, who by this time had sold both it and the house and moved away to a different place far away. The one asset that Ann had been able to legally keep was a $120,000 life insurance policy from Jackie's death before Ann was to go to trial. Ann's former lawyer, Amy G. Dala, had used a legal loophole to prevent the courts from knowing about this payout by placing the cash into a trust fund, which Ann was to draw from once released. By this time, the fund had collected interest and was now up to almost $200,000.

Once out of the prison grounds, Ann hailed a taxi and went to look for a cheap apartment she could rent. Upon finding one just outside of the city, she moved in and began looking for work. It was not easy getting a job for an ex-convict, and Ann was no exception. The handful of jobs she was offered were paid very less and required lots of hours to work. Ann was not interested in intense work with little pay. Even though was not in desperate need of money at the moment, she knew that the 200 grand would not last forever. She was going to give up searching just yet, though, and she kept applying both online and though employment agencies. She searched an searched for days on end, but had no luck.

During Ann's spare times she decided to draw out her plan to take out revenge against the people whom she felt had ruined her life. "These people ruined my life, so I am going to ruin theirs" she told herself as she made the plans. She decided that first place to try and get information on them was through social media. Ann decided to look at their posts for information about themselves as well as any patterns that could help her determine when and where to carry out her plans on them. "Good thing mom and dad are already dead" she mused, "now that will save me a lot or trouble."

The first target on her list was Thad. She combed through the internet for any information on Thad. The only results she could find on Google were the articles that covered him from over 12 years ago after Ann had been arrested and tried. But there were no articles on Thad since Ann's conviction. It also did not help that Thad had no social media pages, save for a LinkedIn account that listed only his credentials, education, and work history. Ann noticed that he was now working for a different company now, one that was based in St. Paul. But there was no information on where Thad lived now. She checked the Yellow Pages website, but the information that the site had listed his old address and phone number. "He can't still be living in that house" said Ann. "It has already been sold. Or perhaps whoever lives in it now might know where he moved to.

Undaunted, Ann decided that the best place to start would be the house that they had lived in. But she soon encountered a major obstacle: she had no vehicle of her own now that she was released. "I cannot afford to take a taxi or an Uber of Lyft" she thought, "Not only is it expensive, but there runs the risk of having unwanted witnesses who will send me right back to prison. Well I am not going to take that chance! I need to get my own car, now!"

The next person on her list was Amy G. Dala. "That bitch ruined everything for me" Ann justified to herself. "She did not get me a female judge. She did not help get released on bail. She did not help me get out of a long prison sentence! That bitch is as good as dead!"

Ann decided to stalk Dala. Ann found out through internet, and through social media, where Dala worked at, though not where she lived. Dala's office was located in an office building in downtown Minneapolis. Across the street was a coffee store. Ann would spend the next few days sitting in the store all day. She would watch out for the attorney

One night, the attorney made her way back to her car. There were several other cars around, but there seemed to be no other people nearby. Once the attorney got in, she put her key in the ignition. Before she could turn it, though, Ann emerged from under the back seat and struck her on the head multiple times with a tire iron. The victim slumped onto the passenger seat, unconscious.

Ann then took a sigh of relief. She had spent a week stalking her first victim, and she was glad to have finally put the first of plans in actions. She looked around to make sure there was still no one else around. When she could see no one else, she put her victim's body onto the passenger seat and drove off. They then came to a river that was just outside the city's borders. They crossed over the bridge and went into a forest. Ann then drove off the road and parked the car close to the edge of the river. After taking the cash out of the attorney's purse, she then placed it around the attorney's body before dragging her and dumping her into the river.

As soon as the river began to carry the body away, Ann went back to the car and drove back to her apartment. The attorney floated on the river for several minutes before regaining consciousness. When she did, she tried to swim or call for help, but she could do neither.

The next day, her body was found floating around by several witnesses. The police and rescue team arrived and hauled her out of the water and into the hospital where she was pronounced dead upon arrival. The autopsy revealed a large amount of water in her lungs, indicating that she died by drowning.

The victim's husband and called the police to report her missing during the previous night when she did not return. Once the body was found, he was devastated emotionally. He went on television to plead for answers for his wife's strange death. Ann was in her apartment that morning, watching the husband on the tv news. As he was struggling to speak and hold back the tears to the reporters, Ann was laughing heartily at his uncontrollable misery.

"Well, well, well. So you are sad that your wife is dead eh? Well, that is what she gets for ruining my life. She was an incompetent bitch who should have never allowed me to spend a day of my life in prison. Because, I never deserved to go to prison. I deserved better everything. Better life. Better husband. Those type of things. But now that your wife has indirectly taken all those things away from me, I will take those things away from her. I'm sorry to have to put you through all this miser of losing your loved one. But I understand. I fell your pain, man. I once was also in a relationship. I thought he was the love of my life. But then, he became a stranger. He was just as good as dead. Maybe he was better of dead, just the way I wanted."

The police began to look for the attorney's car. It was nowhere to be seen at the place where the victim's body was found.

The investigators unofficially assumed that the car may have been dumped in the river, as it was a popular place to dump cars. Although a search was made for the car, no one could identify it. No one had bothered to investigate or question Ann about this. No one had any reason to. There were no witnesses. There were no surveillance cameras on the premises of the lawyer's workplace that could capture the kidnapping and car theft. And that was the just the way Ann wanted it to be.

Later that morning, Ann drove over to the house where she and Thad used to live. Once she pulled into the driveway, she noticed an unfamiliar car parked in the driveway. Ann walked up to the front door and knocked. Seconds later, a man answered it. "Can I help you, ma'am?" he asked.

"Yes. My name is Sarah Penter. And I am here to visit my brother, Thaddaeus. I believe this is his address."

"I am sorry ma'am, but no with that name lives here anymore."

"Would you happen to have his forwarding address?"

"Just a second" he responded before disappearing. He returned seconds later with a folded-up paper and recited the address. Ann thanked then man and quickly went on her way. The address that the man gave was in St. Paul, and Ann wanted to get there as quickly as she could. "I hope the traffic is good at this time of morning" she thought, remembering the good old days when the rush hour traffic would be backed for miles on end.

Finally, after driving for a little over half an hour, Ann arrived at the address, which was a downtown apartment complex. She parked on the street across from the building and went to the front of the complex. She saw a sign beside the door that read: Only Residents Allowed. Visitors Must Sign In At Front Desk. So Ann arrived at the front desk as instructed. A woman was sitting my the receptionist desk. "Good morning!" she called, "Are you a visitor?"

"Yes" replied Ann, "I am looking for a Mr. Thaddeus Penter. Does he live here?"

"Let me see" said the receptionist as she went through the computer database. "Ahh yess! Now Mr. Penter did live here, but he moved out about a year ago."

"Do you have his forwarding address?"

The receptionist once again went through the database. "Um, no, it looks like he never did gives one. I am sorry I cannot help you any further."

"No problem" smiled Ann, "but thanks for your help." And with that Ann went back to her car. Once she was seated, Ann gave a sigh of frustration. She took out her phone and went through it. "Well, as far as his LinkedIn page goes, the company he works for his located here in the city" she said. "So all I have to do is find his place of work, and soon I will find him!"

Ann set her Google Maps over to the address of Thad's workplace. Within minutes, she arrived at the destination. The workplace was a large office building located in downtown. After parking her car, Ann walked inside the building and straight to the front desk. "Excuse me" she said to the receptionist, "but I am looking for Thad Penter."

"I think I can be of assistance to you" said a man standing right next to Ann. "My name is Frank Dess, and I am the senior manager here."

"My name is Sarah" said Ann as they shook hands, "I am here to visit my brother Thad."

"Sure then, you can step into my office. Have a seat. Now then, you are Thad Penter's sister, am I right?"

"Yes. That is right. I haven't seen him in a long time and I would like to see him as soon as I can."

"Ok. But surely you would know where he lives."

"No, I don't. I am afraid we have been apart for a long time. And only now did I know of his existence. We separated as children when our parents separated, and I would like to reunite with him to fulfill my bucket list."

Dess smiled. "Well, I am glad you have finally found out about him. And I think I can help you find him."

"Really? You know where he lives?"

"Well, let's just say that I know he currently lives in New York, if I remember correctly, but I am not sure of his address."

"New York City?" asked Ann eagerly.

"Yes."

"Do you know which part he might be living in?"

"You mean which borough? No, I'm afraid not."

"So all you know is that he lives somewhere in New York, but you don't know where? Well, I guess I'm gonna have to find him on my own. Thank you very much, and have a good day."

Ann then stood up and quickly walked out of the office. Dess watched her exit the building and enter into her car. He tried to get a glimpse of the license plate, but was too far away to get a good look at it. No sooner had Ann left than he placed a call.

"Hello" said the voice on the other end.

"Hello, Thad, this is Frank. Can you spare a moment?"

"Yeah. What's up?"

"Have you got a sister named Sarah?"

"I have no siblings at all."

"All right, now listen to me carefully. A woman just came into the office, claiming to be your sister. But she looks a lot like your ex-wife, Ann."

"Oh no!" gasped Thad. "Is she still there?"

"She just left. I tried to see her license plate number, but I cannot. Where are you now?"

"I'm at home. Oh Frank, I feel so scared for myself. Did you tell her where I live?"

"I told her you live somewhere in New York, but that I did not the address. My guess is she is going to look for you over there in some wild goose chase. But just to be safe, come to work a little later than usual, just to give her some time to get as far away as possible. I will call the police and let them know about this."

"Ok Frank, I appreciate it very much. I still have that restraining order against her. If she is trying to retaliate against me, then she has gotten way too close than she should. This woman is dangerous, Frank. I want nothing to do with her."

"I will inform security about this. In the meantime, take care. Talk to you later. Bye bye!" Dess quickly called the police and the facility security. They too were unable to access the license plate, since the surveillance did not properly capture the plate. They tried to locate Ann but were unable. This made it virtually impossible to serve her a restraining order against going on the buil

Meanwhile, Ann was heading back to her home in Minneapolis. She was fuming that she might not be able to find Thad easily. "That son of a bitch is much harder to find than a needle in a haystack!" she exclaimed. "I was so looking forward to seeing his ugly face and giving him his comeuppance. Now he lives in the Big Apple, where millions of other people live. And eve his own company does not know where he lives. I can go to New York, all right, but where would I look, and where would I even begin to look? Looks like I have to scratch him off of my list But I guess a guy like that is probably not worth finding after all. At least now that I have bigger prizes to set my sights on. Maybe things ain't so bad after all."

CHAPTER 7

Ann soon set her sights up the next target on her list: the prosecutor Garland Springley. She had quite a challenge stalking
him online, as the only account he had was on Facebook, and
even that was the official page for his office. To further com-
plicate matters, he had posted very little about his personal life,
making it hard for Ann to detect patterns in his daily routine.
"No problem" she said to herself, "I can still stalk the good
old-fashioned way."

And she did. After tracking down where he lived, Ann
began to spy on his house that was in a residential area. She
spent her days off from work watching his house. Whenever
he left his house at any time during the day, Ann would follow
him wherever he went. In order to avoid being recognized,
Ann always wore sunglasses and a hat or cap. "If I can't avoid
any witnesses" she told herself, "at the very least I can make
sure that if and when they do talk, they can never give me
away."

During her stalking, she noticed that the target would
often leave during mid-morning and arrive back home after
dark. She also noticed that there seemed to be no one else living
with him. "Perfect!" she said to herself. "That will make my task
even easier! No family means no witnesses!"

Finally, the day came for Ann to put her plan into practice. She waited until Springely left the house at the usual time. As soon as he was out of sight, Ann scoured the area to make sure there were no neighbors or any passersby about. She saw several neighbors walking about, tending their gardens, and engaging in other activities. "Come one, come on!" she groaned. "Hurry up, hurry up! Can't these people finish these things faster? Or at the very least, can they postpone those things until after I leave?"

After waiting several grueling minutes, which almost seemed like hours to her, Ann finally decided that the coast was clear. She slowly got out of her car and took out her purse with her. She kept dodging behind the large trees, just in case anyone was looking. She snuck into his backyard and used a glass cutter to open the backdoor window to access the lock. Once she did that, she unlocked and opened the door.

Once inside, Ann looked all over the inside. She slowly walked all around the house to make sure that there was no one else inside. Upon finding no one else, Ann proceeded to head straight for the fridge and helped herself to whatever she could find. "He won't be needed these once he gets back" she told herself.

After helping herself to whatever her stomach could digest, Ann decided to take a good tour of the house. She started in the living room. She noticed a table and a sofa, along with one of the latest HDTVs nailed to the wall. She decided to help herself to watching some tv to pass the time. For the next hour or so, Ann began channel surfing for something that even remotely interested her. Every so often, Ann would land on a channel and be intrigued by whatever was playing on it. But after a while, she would grow bored and again change the channel.

Pretty soon, Ann grew bored of watching tv and turned it off to look for other activities. She saw some magazines by the sofa and began to read all of them. Although she found them way more interesting, no doubt because of the flashy photos on the pages, Ann soon grew bored soon after that. She began to tour the house once more. This time for anything that might help her pass away the time faster. She came into his room, and began to lightly rummage through it. She went through his dresser. It was full of his clothes. "Nothing interesting here" she told herself.

She went inside his walk-in closet. There were more of his clothes. Many of them were is business suits. Ann rummaged through the clothes, including the pockets, for anything of value that he may have left. Apart from some small amounts of cash, there was nothing in the pockets. After pocketing the cash, Ann decided to have a little fun by wearing some of his clothes. She put on one of his business suits, pranced around like a fashion model on a runway, and stood in front of the large mirror on the dresser.

Next, she put on another one of his suits. This time, Ann took out her phone and started playing the Nancy Sinatra song, "These Boots are Made for Walking" while dancing, prancing, and twerking around while lip-syncing to the lyrics. When she heard the verse "These boots are made for a walkin'/ And that's just what they'll do/One of these days these boots are gonna walk all over you/", Ann stood on the bed and walked all over it.

Ann played around with Springley's clothes for several minutes. She kept this up until she had worn all his clothes and had played the song more than 120 times nonstop. After she was finished, she made sure to neatly put back all of them the way she had found them originally. Afterwards, she lay down on his bed to take some rest. "My, my!" she sighed, "I never had this much fun since I was a child." She was exhausted from all that dancing and decided to take a nap on his bed. As she rested, she took out her charger from her purse to recharge her phone battery.

After resting for a few hours, Ann was starting to get hungry. It was already afternoon by this time. Ann then decided to order a pizza on her phone, and have it delivered to that house. Minutes later, the delivery man arrived. Ann had already paid online with her credit card and took her order. As she was eating it, she couldn't help but wonder about whether the delivery man would identify her once the police started investigating Springely's death.

"I hope I did not make a dreadful mistake. I was supposed to have taken great care to avoid being detected. And now, I have already let my guard slip. No doubt they have my name and credit card information by now. They will likely use this against me. Oh dear! I just have to hope for the best."

After eating the entire pizza, Ann was about to throw the box away, when she decided to find a more creative way to dispose it without leaving any clues to her having ever set foot in that house. She took a match from the fireplace mantle and quickly made her way outside to the backyard. There, on the porch, she looked all over to see if any of the neighbors were around. Upon seeing no one, Ann set the box on fire, right on the porch. Within seconds, the entire cardboard container was turned into pile of curly ashes. Before the fire could spread, Ann made sure to promptly stomp out the fire and scatter the ashes onto the lawn. "The wind should take care of the rest", she mused before heading back inside.

Back inside, Ann decided to look at the family pictures that were scattered around the house. On the living room end table was a picture of the prosecutor at his graduation party. There were a handful of other people in that photo. A couple of them looked pretty old. "Those two must be his parents" said Ann. Other pictures she could locate included people who looked like they could be his siblings or friends. But Ann also noticed that, of the dozen or so photos in the house, not a single one had any indication of the target being married or having any children. There were no such clues elsewhere in the house, either, save for pictures of his parents' wedding and pictures of him as a child. None of the pictures had the target wearing, for example, a wedding ring.

"What a lonely, poor old guy" mused Ann sarcastically. "I'll bet he's lonely. He's got no family of his own. I'll bet that will be a harder for him to avoid what is coming to him tonight. I'd be willing to bet that, after tonight, his family will be in for a surprise of their lives when I'm done with him."

By this time evening had fallen. And it was soon just starting to get dark. Ann knew from stalking her target that he would very likely be arriving after dark. As the minutes became hours, the house began to get dark. Ann wanted to turn on the lights, but was afraid that the neighbors, or even the target, would spot her. She instead decided to be in parts of the house that still had some sunlight shining through the windows. But pretty soon, that turned out to be futile as the sun was setting. Ann then decided to use her phone's flashlight to navigate her way around the interior once darkness fully settled.

Ann knew that this was the chance to keep a sharp lookout for her target to arrive. She waited patiently for him to arrive, periodically checking her phone for the time. Finally, a familiar car pulled into the driveway. Ann quickly gathered her purse and other belongings, silenced her phone, and slowly walked upstairs into the bedroom and into the closet. As Springely made his way to the front door, he noticed a burnt smell coming from his backyard. "Must have been the neighbors barbecuing, or perhaps burning their yard waste" he said. Minutes later, he came slowly inside and turned on the light within his room and began to take off his business clothes and place them on his bed.

Ann quietly watched from a small opening in the door. The target had his back towards the closet, and the mirror on his dresser was perpendicular to him, so he couldn't see anyone come up from behind him. Ann then decided, as a precaution, to put on one of his business coats on. She then slowly put down her purse and took out of it a pair of thick garden gloves. After putting them on, she then took out a long string of barbed wire and held onto it on both ends. She slowly walked out of the closet and towards him. "Good thing this floor is carpeted" she thought, "or else he could hear me and make my task very hard."

As the target was starting to take off his pants, Ann wrapped the wire around his neck as tight as she could! Springley screamed in surprise, fear, and pain as the blood oozed out of his neck and onto the floor and the coat that Ann was wearing. Ann kept on tightening her grip on her target, but kept fighting back by trying to yank himself out of her grip. Ann then started to drag him all over the room and bash his head against the wall repeatedly.

After the two struggled for several minutes, the prosecutor fell to the floor. Ann checked him for any signs of breathing but could not detect any. She then sat down on the bed to catch her breath. After staring at him for several minutes, Ann went back into the closet, reached into her purse, and took out a large knife. She then went over to the target's body, pulled down his underpants, cut off his large penis, and placed it in a plastic bag. Then she took off the coat she had put on and covered it over the area his genitilia area. "Son of a bitch ruined a nice jacket!" she said sarcastically.

Ann then placed the gloves, knife and wire into her purse. She then washed off the blood from the bag and then placed it inside her pockets. She then made her way into the backyard. But before she could get to the gate separating the front yard to the back yard, the neighbor's dog began barking loudly at Ann.

Ann was horrified at the dog. Partly out of fear for her safety, but also primarily because she could see the lights inside the house, and feared the barking would draw attention to her. "Think, think, think!!" she hissed to herself. Then she had an idea. Ann quickly took out the plastic bag, opened it up, and tossed into the neighbor's yard. As the dog was silently devouring the severed penis, Ann made her way back to her car without any more problems.

On the way back, Ann was gloating about her latest accomplishment, though she was very upset at having to dispose her souvenir. "That stupid mutt" she grumbled as she drove, "I was going to send that penis to his living relatives. I was hoping to see their horrified faces on the news, and talk about how they are so scared and sad about what happened to their precious loved one. And I went through so much trouble just to obtain that prize, too! Ah well, I guess these things happen. But on the bright side, two gone, two more to go!"

On the way back, Ann stopped at the edge of a lake just off the highway, and dumped her purse in. The weight of the knife that was inside the purse caused it to sink fast. After watching to make sure it completely went underwater, Ann drove back home and went promptly to bed.

CHAPTER 8

The next target on Ann's hit list was her sister Emma. As usual, she began by poring through her social media accounts. Ann could tell by the some of the pictures that Emma posted that she had lived in the same house as before Ann went to prison. "Well, well, well" gloated Ann, "looks like little sister has made big sister's task really easy!"

But there had been some very important changes in Emma's life after all. By looking at her LinkedIn profile, Ann discovered that Emma had been promoted just a few years earlier to senior correspondent for Sportsmanship. On both the company website and on Emma's own Facebook page, she had been given several awards and recognition for her journalistic work, especially for covering and revealing many major stories in the world of sports.

Another major change in Emma's life was that, just a few years after Ann was convicted, Emma had married a man. His LinkedIn profile listed him as both an art dealer and an antiques dealer. He had no other social media profiles of his own. But he was featured prominently in his wife's many posts.

In many of Emma's posts, particularly on certain days such as birthdays, wedding anniversaries, Thanksgiving, and Valentine's day, she would often post romantic pictures of the two of them and write captions gushing about how much she loved her husband and would often place heart emojis on those posts. She would often post about how marrying him was one of the best decisions of her life, how much he meant to her, how she cannot imagine living without him, and optimism for a bright future together.

After scrolling through all of these romantic posts, Ann was fuming with anger and jealousy. "Not only does my bitchy sister wreck my entire life, but she also gets to live a much better life than ever before! Better job! Better husband!! Better everything!!! Everything that I never had but deserved to have! So she is happy with her life, eh?! And she cannot imagine living on without her precious man?! And she wants to live with him forever, huh?! Well, it takes two to make a marriage, but only one to break it!!"

The following weekend, Ann set out to Emma's house. The house was located in suburban Chicago, so it would take her several hours to arrive. She started early that morning to avoid the heavy rush hour traffic and arrived in Emma's neighborhood by noon. She parked her car several houses down the street from Emma's and watched her house from a distance. She could see Emma's car parked on the driveway but could see no one inside either the car or the house. She waited and waited to see any sign of her sister coming out of the house.

The hours passed. Ann kept watching the house. As she waited and watched, her mind started to wander off to the past, when she first visited Emma at that house many years ago. This was a few years after Ann had married Thad. The then-married coupled arrived that day, along with Ann and Emma's parents. Emma had recently moved in after taking out a mortgage on that house.

"I'm so glad that my baby girl has finally got a place of her own to stay in", said their mother as they all sat in the living room. "I was afraid that maybe your first job would not be enough and that you would need to have your father and I, as well as Ann and Thad here, pitch in and give you some more money for this house."

Emma smiled. "Well, if I did not get that pay raise, and if Thad was not kind enough to find a mortgage plan that was just right for me, then I would still very well be living in that cheap, cramped, downtown apartment complex. Not to mention I would probably be on my hands and knees begging all of you guys to give me money!"

They all laughed. "Oh don't get me wrong" she continued while chuckling, "I love this city. It has so many great things about it. But I just don't feel safe living all by myself in downtown. I much prefer here in the suburb, where I can live just away from all the noise and bustle and enjoy the trees and the birds and flowers. There is so much space here, and that is just what I need!"

"I am so glad that my baby has gotten what she wanted" replied Kent, "but speaking of living all by yourself, when are you going to settle down like your sister?"

"Whenever I want to!" declared Emma. "I have just gotten my life in order. I'll tie the knot whenever I'm in the mood for it."

"If you want some advice on finding your true love, or how to live once you have found one, then Ann is probably your best source" said Thad as he placed his arm around his bride. Ann reciprocated the gesture. "Actually" she replied, "if you really advice on how to deal with your significant other, you can ask this fine gentleman."

Ann suddenly awoke from her daydreaming. She looked back at the house. There was still no sign of Emma or her husband anywhere. Then, minutes later, Ann spotted a mailvan making its way towards that house. She thought nothing of it at first. But as the van drew nearer and nearer to the mailbox at Emma's house, Ann had an idea some into her head. She watched the mailman put the mail in the box and drive away. Minutes later, he disappeared around a bend off in the distance. Several more minutes passed before Ann saw Emma walk out of the house and stroll towards the mailbox.

Ann had waited for this moment to arrive. She put on her sunglasses and cap. Then she turned on her engine and slowly drove forwards towards the house. As soon as Emma was standing on the road in front of the mailbox, Ann sped and crashed right into Emma, who let out a short but loud scream. The impact caused Emma to be flung several feet away an onto the road. The impact also made the bones in her hips, ribs, and back snap like toothpicks.

Emma landed on the road unconscious. Ann then positioned her left front wheel so that it would roll over her head and crush her skull. As Ann drove away, Emma's husband came running out of the house. He saw the car drive off, but could not see the license plate properly. He then saw Emma's lifeless, bloodied body on the ground. The tire marks on her clothes were visible. He rushed over, embraced her body, and began sobbing and screaming uncontrollably as some of the neighbors, who had witnessed the tragedy, came over and tried to console him.

As Ann drove off, she was excited at having accomplished her task so easily and quickly. By the time she had arrived back to her apartment, it was already nearing dark. Ann was still in very high spirits as she crawled into her bed. She couldn't help but laugh at the anticipation of how Emma's widower was going to take it all.

The next morning, Ann turned on the news. As she had expected, Emma's widower was on the news, telling reporters about what he witnessed and how devasted he was. As he was struggling to hold back the tears, Ann could not help but cackle at his pain. The more the man cried, the more Ann laughed. After she turned off the tv, Ann began to taunt him with her thoughts as she laid back on her bed.

"Oh, you poor, sweet, precious man you. Did you lose the love of your life? The woman of your dreams? The one who kept posting all about you on social media and telling the world how much she loved you and how much you meant to her? The one who said that she could not live without you? Are you sad that someone like that has been taken away from you so soon?

"Well, man, I am deeply, very sorry to have taken away your precious bride. But you see, she had it coming to her. She deserved what she got. You see, before you married her, she was my sister and my best friend. When we were just girls, she was my only friend. We were so close to each other. We both thought that there was nothing in this big old world that could get between us. We were as close as sisters could be, even after we were all grown up and had our own jobs and friends, and love interests.

"But then, one day, that all changed. It was on that day, a few years back before you married her, that I told your precious little Emma that I had a problem, and I wanted her to help me get out of it quickly. I explained what that problem was, and how she could help me out like the way a good sister should have. But it was then that, for some reason, the Emma I had known for such a such a long time and thought would be the one person I could turn to in my time of need, well, she turned out to be a selfish little coward. She refused to help me. She said that it was too risky. She said that she did not think it was the right thing to do. Like the bitch she has always been, she would not help her loving, older sister.

"But then, a few days later, she called me out of the blue, and said that she had changed her mind. I was so elated! I thought it was great that my little sister and best friend had finally come to her senses and wanted to help out big sister after all! I was so glad, and I began to tell her of my plans. And she listened carefully. Then we set out to put my plan in action.

"But just as we were putting the plan in action, I realized that it was all a ruse. Emma dear did not really want to help me after all. She had set up a trap, and lead me to walk straight into it. I was devastated then, and I have been devasted since then. She had betrayed me and had me locked up for six years, all because I wanted to improve my life, and she wanted to ruin it all for me.

"And to make matters worse, as I was languishing in prison year after year, day after day, Emma was enjoying life like she never had before. She had gotten a promotion, and a husband, yourself. It was so unfair! After all she had done, she got away with it while I was left on the short end of the stick. I deserved a better job and a better husband, not that bitch!

"I still cannot believe or get over what she had done to me. I now find it hard to know whom I can or cannot trust. And your Emma darling is to blame. That is why I set out to get payback on her. But you will never understand this. And I hope that you never find out about this, because I want you to spend the rest of your life in severe depression over losing your loved one. You will grow insane by having all your questions unanswered. Your life will be a living hell for as long as you live.

"But you want to know something? I think that you also deserved what happened to Emma. After all, I warned her many years ago that someday she would find a man and fall in love with him. But sooner or later, she would find him to be boring and useless. What if you were already boring and useless? What if she was growing tired of your mere presence? What if you were cheating on her behind her back? Suppose that the man of her dreams was nothing more than a snake? I know because I was had a husband like that. I loved him because I thought he was good. Then I realized that he was a worthless loser who only loved big trucks. Maybe you are just like Mack. Perhaps you were becoming a worthless loser too. Perhaps you deserved to not have a loving wife anymore. Perhaps I did your bride a big favor by saving her the misery of living long enough to see you turn into a worthless snake. She ought to be glad that I did this to her. You cannot trust men at all. I know because I married one."

Later that afternoon, Ann heard a knock on her door. She looked out the peephole and saw a man and a woman dressed in business suits and sunglasses and standing outside. She opened the door. "Can I help you two?" she smiled as she greeted them.

"Are you Ms. Ann Noyd?" asked the woman.

"Yes I am."

"I am Heather Corland, and this is Ron Jepper, we're with the FBI." They flashed their badges. "Can we come in?"

"Yes" replied Ann as she let them in and gestured them to sit on the sofa as she pulled up a chair. "Now what can I help you two with?" she asked while still smiling.

"Ms. Noyd" said Jepper, "we are here with regards to your sister, Emma."

Ann's smile turned into a look of concern. "Yes? What of her?" she asked. "Is she in trouble of some kind?"

"Yes she has been" replied Corland, "and a very tragic one too. Just yesterday evening, she was run over by a car while she was getting the mail from her mailbox."

Ann then gave a look of horror and gasped. "Oh my goodness. Is she alright?"

"No" said Jepper, "she apparently died instantly. When the medics arrived, they could not detect a pulse. She had hemorrhaged during the time it took for the medics to arrive."

"Oh no!" Ann gasped again while shedding crocodile tears. "Who could have done this to such a great person like Emma?"

"We are looking for the answers right now" said Corland. "We thought maybe you could help us."

"Anything I can do to help at all?" sniffed Ann.

"When did you last speak to your sister?" asked Jepper.

"Well" hesitated Ann, "well, um, we spoke frequently. We were so close. I know I spoke to her just a few days ago. I think the last time was just a couple of days ago, maybe a week ago, no more than a week. Yeah, that's right, about a week ago. We talked and talked for hours. We had such a great time." Ann then bowed her head down and sniffled, though she was really trying to hide her glee at her sister's death. Seconds later, she lifted up her head back up towards the agents.

"What exactly did the two of you talk about?" asked Jepper.

"Well, we spoke about many things" Ann stammered.

"Like what?" asked Corland.

Ann paused for a few seconds as she scrambled to think of what to make up next. "Well, we spoke about sister stuff."

"Sister stuff?" asked a puzzled Jepper.

"Yeah" replied Ann, "you know, stuff that sisters talk about. You know, about growing up together back in the good ol' days when we were young and carefree and when life was much more simpler back then. And how now that we are adults we are constantly burdened by responsibilities like family and work and stuff. And we had such a good time while we spoke."

She paused to wipe off the fake tears. "Well who could have done such a terrible thing like that to my sweet little sister? She never did anything to deserve this! She never had a single enemy in her entire short life!!"

"Now, now" said Corland, "like I said, we are still looking into the matter, as it just happened yesterday and we need to get hold of some information before we can come to a conclusion. Now first of all, where were you yesterday evening?"

"I was here" replied Ann.

"All day?" asked Jepper.

"All day".

"Was there anyone with you?" asked Corland.

"No. I was here all by myself. And now I'm gonna be all by self forever now that my sister's gone."

"Looks like it will be that way" mused Jepper as he hastily wrote in his notebook.

"Now then Ms. Noyd" said Corland, "how well have you known your brother-in-law?"

"Emma's husband?" asked Ann. The detectives nodded. "Well, not that much. I never spoke to him. I mean, I did occasionally whenever we visited, and I did have his phone number. And I did speak to him just this morning. He seemed very upset. He was hysterical and heartbroken. It looks like he will be miserable now that he will be living all by himself now."

"Well Ms. Noyd" said Corland as she and Jepper stood up, "we will be on this case. And if anything turns up, just be sure to call us on the number listed on the card that Jepper is giving you. You have a good day now."

After the agents had left, Ann began dancing around her apartment in joy. "Yes! Yes! Yes!" she laughed, "I'm in the clear now. Yahoooooo!!! They don't suspect me in the slightest! I'm freeee!!"

As the agents drove away, they mused over their visit. "What do you make of it?" asked Corland while she drove their car.

"Well" her partner sighed, "It does kinda point to her as a probable culprit. I mean, we both know that Ann Noyd had a criminal conviction for attempting to murder her then-husband, so it is very likely she would have done the same to her sister. And the fact that Emma herself tipped off the police about Ann's plans gives Ann a motive for wanting her sister dead."

"Revenge" said Corland ominously. "That woman is dangerous. I don't think she has been, or ever will be, honest with us or anyone else for that matter."

"Right you are! And by the way, she said that she spoke to Emma's husband just this morning. But according to the man himself, he never spoke to Ann at all. He said he never visited her and that he did not know where she lived. He did not even know that Emma had a sister until recently. I'm sure by now he has done a Google search on Ann and probably knows everything. And of course, we checked the victim's cell phone records. She ceased talking with Ann after Ann was arrested for attempted murder.

"Yes" said Corland, "I agree with all that, although I don't know if he would be in a mood to research about his sister-in-law now since he is too busy grieving Emma's death. You know, it is all so strange that Ann claimed to have visited him and spoken to him, but never once mentioned him by name. I think she herself has done it, or else had a confederate do it for her."

"Indeed she may have" concurred Jepper. "But do you think we should get a search warrant for her vehicle and possibly even her apartment? I think we might find a clue or two to nail her on it."

"That would be a good idea, but I doubt we could obtain one at the moment. Right now, Ann Noyd is only a person of interest. I doubt we can obtain a warrant at this moment, since there does not seem to be enough probable cause to search her car. And even if we did search her car, what guarantee is there that we will have found something to use against Ann

Noyd? Sure it will likely exonerate her, but it will have wasted our time."

Sure enough, they were indeed denied a warrant for that very reason. But searching the vehicle would have indeed been helpful. It had deep dents on its bumper and front bender as a result of hitting Emma.

CHAPTER 9

The last, but not least, target on Ann's list was the retired judge, Warren Peese, himself. She had saved him for last. "This son of bitch is gonna get the worst punishment of them all!" she squealed with glee while making up her plans. As with the other three, she first scoured through his social media profiles.

But Ann soon ran into an obstacle. The judge had no social media presence, save for a LinkedIn page, which listed him as a senior partner in a prominent law firm.

But apart from his age and credentials, Ann could gather nothing else about him. "No matter" she mused, "I'm sure the Yellow Pages website would help." And indeed it did. Within minutes, she had found his address on the site.

With all this at her disposal, Ann set about to stalk her target for the next few days. She would park near his house during the mornings, follow him to his place of work, and then follow him back to his house. She made sure to check what times he departed and arrived back home.

Ann also noticed one key detail in her observations. Even though the judge was wearing a wedding ring, there was no one else to be seen inside his house. She never saw anyone else enter or leave that house. "So he must be either getting a divorce, or just widowed" Ann speculated. "Or perhaps she is away for now. Well in that case, it makes my job a lot easier now that there won't be any witnesses to deal with. But the sooner I get this over with, the better."

One night, after stalking him for 3 consecutive days, Ann had become impatient and decided to make her move. She parked close to his house and waited for him to arrive. Less than an hour later, a familiar car pulled into the driveway. Out of it stepped a gray-haired man in his early seventies, wearing his golf shirt and khaki pants. Ann quickly got out of the car, taking along a shoebox and a large knife. As the judge was making his way to the front door, Ann quietly made her way through his lawn and waited just around the corner of the front lawn. While waiting, she slowly took out of the shoebox a pair of high heels and put them on. Then she put her sneakers into the box. As soon as he opened the door, Ann rushed over and kicked him into his house, closed the door behind her, and deadbolted it. When the judge turned around, Ann dropped the shoebox, grabbed him by his collar, and pressed the blade of the knife onto his neck.

"Hello, judgy! Remember me?!"

Judge Peese stared at Ann and was breathing heavily and all shaken-up. "A-Ann Noyd. I'll never forget you from all those years."

"And I will never forget you, you old bastard! Now I have just completed a dozen depressing years in prison.

"And you deserved every one of them!"

"Shut up!" she screamed as she slapped him across the face. "You ruined my life! And I want payback for what you did to me! My family has disowned me! My friends have deserted me! I can't get my old job back! I am stuck working in a lousy job! And you are responsible for wrecking all this misery! All I wanted was a better life for myself! I wanted to escape my boring life, my boring husband, and my boring job! And now I have nothing! You have ruined my life forever, you pedophile!!"

"What makes you think I am a pedophile?"

"Because you fucked me when I was younger with a long and unfair prison sentence! You destroyed my life by throwing me behind bars. You are no better than a rapist! A child molester!! A motherfucker!!! And you will pay for all this!!"

"Just because you wanted a better life for yourself did not mean that you should have your husband murdered!"

"He deserved to die! He was useless, boring, good for nothing! Just like all men! All he did was go to his stupid job day after day. He never left me alone! I wanted some freedom, but he kept getting in the way! I just wanted to get away from it all, but you have taken everything away from me you son of a bitch!!! And now you will pay for what you have done!!"

Unknown to Ann, after she placed the knife against him, the judge had secretly and quickly dialed 911 on his cell phone which was in his pocket. The operator had listened to just about the entire conversation. Then she put in a call to the local police department explaining the situation.

Meanwhile, Ann made a cut on the side of the judge's neck. Blood began to trickle from it. Ann then pressed it as hard as she could. The judge screamed, and Ann laughed maniacally. Then she kicked him in the crotch. As he lay on the ground in pain, Ann began raining kicks on him with her shoes. She had selected them specifically for their heaviness, and the sharpness of the heels. She kicked him and kicked him viscously in the head and chest. Blood spattered all over the floor. Ann kicked him until the heels snapped off and got stuck in his body.

Peese's advanced age and physical fragility was something Ann was eager to take advantage of and did not want to show any mercy to him. She put on her sneakers and dragged him around the house until she found an ironing box. Upon plugging it in, she turned up to the highest setting and was searing his face, neck and chest with it. The judge screamed loudly as his body was getting covered with third degree burns. Ann laughed heartily at his pain.

When the ironing box ran out of water, Peese tried to break free as Ann tried to look for more water. But every time he got to a door or window, Ann would yank him back and continue to torture him. Next up, she started biting both of his ears until her jaw ached. Peese continued to scream. Next Ann took off her belt and started to strangle him. She kept strangling him until he passed out and nearly die. Then she tossed cold water on him and brought him back to his senses.

Ann then dragged him to the nearest doorway. She placed him down and started slamming the door onto him repeatedly. She slammed furiously until she thought it would break from its hinges and fall off. Meanwhile her victim kept yelling in pain and begging for his life. Ann took no notice and continued raining blows on him.

She again placed the belt around his neck and dragged him upstairs. The judge kept trying to break free from her, but it was futile for him. He kept begging her to stop the torture, but it fell on deaf ears.

Finally, Ann dragged him all the way into his bedroom and to the master bathroom. Once they were both inside, she locked the door. There were no windows inside, so Peese was trapped between Ann and the shower stall behind him with its doors closed. Ann then grabbed the judge and made him lean against the closed doors of the shower. Then she repeatedly punched him in the face and chest until he fell backwards, breaking the glass doors and falling into the stall. The glass pieces flew everywhere, some landing in his skin, others in his hair.

Ann then pounced onto him like a leopard pouncing on an antelope. She started biting his nose, wriggling it furiously as he screamed in pain. Then, with a mighty heave, she tore off his nose, spat it into the toilet, and flushed it down! Peese screamed as blood was gushing out of his face and out of Ann's mouth!

Ann then turned on the shower faucet and took out the detachable showerhead. She began to spray cold water onto him. The judge screamed in terror as the bloodied water spattered all over the stall walls and swirled down the drain. Ann kept waterboarding him for several minutes. Then she turned off the showerhead. The judge was whimpering in pain and hypothermia. His skin was starting to turn blue as his teeth were chattering. "Oh I'm so sorry, Goldilocks" Ann said sarcastically, "was that too cold for you. Here, I will make it just right for you." She then turned the setting all the way to hot, and once again sprayed him. The judge screamed even louder has the burning hot water scalded him all over his body, especially his open wounds.

Just then, the judge's wife Natasha pulled into the driveway. She had been out of town during that entire week to attend her high school reunion. Upon entering her house, she saw an empty shoebox, a pair of broken high heel shoes, the broken ironing box, and some blood all on the floor. "Honey!" she called out but got no response. She then saw a trail of blood going all the way upstairs. She followed it, taking care to tiptoe around the blood.

Once she followed it into the master bedroom, the trail stopped in front of the bathroom. She heard her husband screaming and a female voice laughing while the shower was running. She knocked on the door several times but still got no response. She then went over to the dresser, took out a spare key, and opened up the door.

Once she opened it, she was greeted by a gust of hot steam that stung her eyes. After wiping her eyes, she saw the shocking site before her and screamed "Oh my God!!" Ann turned around. She was not expecting anyone else to be in the house. Natasha's unexpected presence interfered with Ann's plans to murder the judge. Ann then sprayed the hot water onto her. Natasha screamed and backed out. Once she wiped the water from her eyes, she saw Ann charging at her with a knife, snarling like a wolf while blood was dripping from her mouth and making her look like a vampire.

Natasha dashed downstairs as Ann chased after her and managed to get back in her car and try to start it. But Natasha was so shaken with fear that she was unable to quickly place her key into the ignition. Ann used the large knife to smash the window and spray glass all over Natasha, who then tried to turn on the ignition. Ann then tried to reach for the keys, and the two women scuffled. Natasha screamed as Ann repeatedly slashed her face and arms.

Just then, they both heard a siren. They looked up and saw a police cruiser heading towards the driveway. It had arrived in response to the judge's secret 911 call. Ann soon ran back inside the house and deadbolted the front door just as another cruiser was making its way to the driveway.

Ann peered through the windows. "Just the way I wanted it!" she sneered sarcastically. "I got the wife to get rid of, but now the cops are swarming at my ass like a pack of wolves." She quickly ran out the back door and thought about heading back to her car. But in order to do that, she would have to go around to the front of the house and past the officers. "No doubt they all got guns" she thought, "I only have a knife. I don't stand a chance against them."

She quickly headed over to the fence and started climbing it. The fence was wooden and slick, but she managed to get over it just before one of the cops could arrive. But upon landing on the other side, Ann severely fractured her ankle. She hissed and groaned in agony, trying not to let anyone hear her. She tried to locate her knife, but had lost it while climbing and could not find it in the dark. Unable to stand, Ann started to painfully slither on the ground like a snake.

Ann did not realize that the noises she made when she hit the ground had awoken the neighbor's four dogs that were sleeping on the backyard porch. They were a German Shepherd, a rottweiler, a Doberman Pincher, and a pit bull. The canine quartet, all of whom were female, watched Ann slither by. Then they started growling before running after her, barking furiously.

Ann could hear the dogs barking, but she could not see where they were coming from. Their barking echoed all around the open space, so they sounded like they were heading in all directions. Before Ann could think of something to avoid them, the dogs started biting all over her body, tearing it to pieces. She screamed for her life in terror and agony.

The cops who had been in the judge's backyard heard the commotion. They flashed their lights onto the neighbor's back-yard. Upon seeing what was happening, they rushed around the fence and made their way to the backyard. The commotion also awoke the dogs' owners, a married couple that lived in the house. They looked out their bedroom window but could see nothing clearly. So they took out their flashlights and dog whistles, turned on the outside lights, and headed out the back door. They saw what was going on and blew their dog whistles. The dogs retreated back to their owners, just as the cops were arriving, leaving behind a bloody, mangled corpse.

About the Author

Joshua Lakhamraju is the son of Indian immigrants. He currently lives in metro Atlanta.